PRAISE FOR KRISSY KNEEN

Praise for *The Adventures of Holly White and the Incredible Sex Machine*

'The combination of sexual awakening, secret societies, and lost technology, wrapped up in Kneen's loving treatment of her subject, character, and story, makes for a remarkably pleasing read. The conclusion is wildly imaginative and surprisingly satisfying. The characters are delightfully varied, including many from groups that are underrepresented in erotic fiction, and each is more fascinating than the last... Kneen encourages the reader to delight in sexuality that is by turns innocent, gleeful, and cheerfully obscene.'
Publishers Weekly US (starred review)

'A hilarious joyride that nods to a wide array of erotic literature.' *Book Riot* US

'I have long been an admirer of the work of Brisbane writer Krissy Kneen, who I believe is one of Australia's hidden literary gems. With each new book, I find myself hoping that readers will finally discover her quirky, sexy and incredibly beautiful writing...A riotous romp through the imagination of one of Australia's most accomplished sex writers.' *Books+Publishing*

'Kneen's outrageous erotic imagination fuels Holly's sexcapades but at its molten X-rated core, this explicit novel is a celebration of the lust for literature as much as for physical debauchery.' Caroline Baum, *Booktopia*

'Kneen once again shows her mastery.' *Daily Telegraph*

'Krissy Kneen writes about sex with nipple-stiffening zest. Her latest is consistently lewd and amusing.' *Brisbane Times*

'A joyful and ambitious mix of science fiction, coming-of-age, adventure story, literary fiction and, of course, erotica. It revels unselfconsciously in bringing these different elements together and is always playful and quirky.' *Australian*

'Like a love-child of Barbarella and the Brave New World, it's a refreshingly confrontational mix of sci-fi surrealism, sexual stirring and erotic honesty.' *Stuff* NZ

'Nobody writes sex like Kneen...her finest book to date.' *Q Weekend*

'It's a rare book that seems to drift like smoke away from the printed page to rewrite the physical world...[Kneen] wants us to strip naked and be transformed.' *Melbourne Review of Books*

Praise for *Steeplechase*

'Kneen's dark imagination and sharp intellect give her erotic writing an edgy quality that reminds the reader, with a genuine shock of recognition, of what sex can be like at its most extreme: ravenous, dangerous, chaotic and transformative.' *Sydney Morning Herald*

'With her most recent work [Kneen] has cemented her place as an author to be read because of the promise, sensual or otherwise, signified by her name on the spine.' *Australian*

'Krissy Kneen's deceptively simple prose careens towards a startling and horrifying denouement; her talent for strikingly vibrant imagery shines...Her fans will continue to relish Kneen's vivid imagery and fearless prose.' *Books+Publishing*

'Absorbing writing with a menacing undertow that drags the reader deep inside a dysfunctional, disturbing relationship.' *Hoopla*

‘Densely plotted and compelling...an accomplished work that will not easily be forgotten.’ *Advertiser*

‘A compelling tale with a brilliant climax...hypnotic, powerful, stirring.’ *BookMooch*

‘The voice is strong, the writing vivid, the prose disarmingly frank...Verdict: Lyrical, persuasive and intriguing.’ *Courier-Mail*

‘Understated and potent. Kneen’s restrained prose is elegant in its simplicity.’ *Australian Book Review*

‘A strange and intricate work that, like any excellent work of art, creates its own tight world whose engine is anxiety and suppression.’ *Age*

Praise for *Affection: a memoir of love, sex and intimacy*

Shortlisted, Queensland Premier’s Award for non-fiction 2010

Shortlisted, Biography of the Year, Australian Book Industry Awards 2010

‘Sex in *Affection* is well written, but it’s the contemplation in between that really shines. Insightful, evocative and bluntly, but never gratuitously, honest...Sexy, sad and deeply satisfying.’ Emily Maguire, *Age*

‘Sexy and beautifully written...An unforgettable book.’ James Frey

‘To focus on the prurient aspects of this memoir... is to miss its gorgeous heart.’ *Courier-Mail*

‘A rare feat...Beneath the surface sexuality, *Affection*’s triumph is that of an assured novelist of any genre.’ *Sunday Age*

'*Affection* is that rare beast: a sexual memoir that is not only uniquely interesting and daringly explicit but is also poetic, offbeat, confronting and funny.'
Linda Jaivin, *Australian*

Praise for *Triptych*

'This is an astounding look at different sorts of love and Kneen is, above all, a sensualist.' *Adelaide Advertiser*

'With nods to Anaïs Nin and Vladimir Nabokov, Kneen writes with tenderness, joy and delight...Delightful, courageous and juicy.' *Big Issue*

ALSO BY KRISSY KNEEN

Affection: a memoir of love, sex and intimacy
Triptych
Steeplechase
The Adventures of Holly White and the Incredible Sex Machine

Krissy Kneen is a Brisbane writer. Her memoir *Affection* was shortlisted for the Queensland Premier's Literary Award in the non-fiction category and for the ABIA award for biography. In 2014 she won the Thomas Shapcott Poetry Prize for her collection *Eating My Grandmother.*

www.furiousvaginas.com
@krissykneen

AN UNCERTAIN GRACE

KRISSY KNEEN

TEXT PUBLISHING MELBOURNE AUSTRALIA

textpublishing.com.au

The Text Publishing Company
Swann House
22 William Street
Melbourne Victoria 3000
Australia

First published in 2017 by The Text Publishing Company

Book design by Imogen Stubbs
Cover photograph by Brandon Willis
Typeset in Sabon 12/18 by J & M Typesetting

Printed and bound in Australia by Griffin Press, an accredited ISO/NZS 1401:2004 Environmental Management System printer

National Library of Australia Cataloguing-in-Publication entry
Creator: Kneen, Krissy, 1968- author.
Title: An uncertain grace / by Krissy Kneen.
ISBN: 9781925355987 (paperback)
9781925410358 (ebook)
Subjects: Australians--Fiction.
National characteristics, Australian--Fiction.

This book is printed on paper certified against the Forest Stewardship Council® Standards. Griffin Press holds FSC chain-of-custody certification SGS-COC-005088. FSC promotes environmentally responsible, socially beneficial and economically viable management of the world's forests.

For Anthony,
from now into the future,
in any incarnation of ourselves,
with love.

PART 1
CASPAR

'FIRST PERSON IS a very narrow and limiting point of view.'

Jane looks up, half-smiles. Her fingers scuttle over her keyboard. It looks like she is listening, typing down every breath of the wisdom I am imparting. Only minutes ago I held a copy of *The Year of Magical Thinking* in my hand, tilting the crisp pale jacket towards the class to display the marketing department's monochrome vision, and they all glanced, all nodded. But when I took a slow walk up the aisle and looked down at Jane's computer, there was the familiar blue Facebook F in the corner of the screen and a chat-box open in the bottom right. I couldn't see the words but the sentiment was clear. Caspar Greenwald does not hold my attention.

'If an author uses first person, a reader is trapped in her or his perspective. You can only learn new information when your character learns it. And most limiting of all? First person, present tense.' I pause, as if deciding whom to call on; as if I didn't already know. 'Jane? Can you tell us why?'

Jane's smile is open, unaffected, the smile of a multitasker. She pauses in her Facebook conversation, moving her hands to surreptitiously angle the screen of her laptop down.

'Because you only know things your character knows as he finds them out himself?'

'Thank you, Jane.'

She grins and adjusts her laptop so that she can see the full screen again. Her fingers return to the keyboard; I imagine the words flashing up on the screen. Sorry. Dr Greenwald is so boring. Her own narrative, first person, present tense.

I often have trouble remembering the names of the students on the first day. I draw a map of the classroom and write names next to the corresponding chairs. This rarely works. The students shift around to participate in group work, evading their identities for the duration of the exercise, and then by the next class they have forged alliances with other students and swapped chairs to sit, like with like. Jane's was the first name I remembered. It was easy. Plain Jane, I thought when she first raised her hand as I read down the class list. She used the raised hand to flick her long dark hair away from her face. She was wearing bright red lipstick and a dress that plunged down towards a thick gold belt, revealing just a hint of lacy red bra easing out towards the perfect V of her neckline. Plain Jane she is not.

Yet the nickname has stuck as surely as my attention, which constantly tracks her movements around the room. If I could tell this story in third person, past tense, I would foreshadow the delicious transgression of our sexual relationship. But no matter how impatient my nature, I am stuck fast in my glacial journey, pinned to my own point of view.

'First person, present tense, or past tense,' I say, trying not to address my words solely towards Jane, 'are the preferred voices for memoir, but—and I stress *but*—they are not the only voices available to you for this genre. Does anyone have any examples of memoirs that stray from the norm in this regard?'

A young Indian student in a paisley shirt raises his hand. Patel? Maybe that was the Indian student in last semester's class. 'Yes,' I nod, leaving him nameless.

'*Boyhood*. J. M. Coetzee.'

'You, sir, have been reading your course dossier.' Everyone utters the required laugh. 'Turn to page nineteen of the dossier.' I allow myself the indulgence of watching Jane lean to her side, reaching into her satchel, the spill of her flesh, the waterfall of her hair. I try to imagine the ineluctable future in which I have grown tired of watching her. When her flesh holds no mystery for me and her perfume is nothing but a background odour, like opening the door to the tedium of your own home after an exciting overseas trip.

It is impossible to think that far ahead while she is still leaning, still rummaging, still swelling out of her perennially low-cut top. Not only can I imagine sleeping with her, it seems inevitable. At this point I am still boring her; still unattractively middle aged. But we haven't got to Rabelais yet. The bacchanal is still to come.

*

The envelope has been slipped through the slot in my door, the memory stick so thin I can barely feel it through the textured card. Liv still uses good quality stationery. It is one of the first things that attracted me to her. Her assignment printed on heavy cream paper with a faint watermark on each page.

Compared with Jane, Liv was less memorable in the flesh, more subtle. She didn't stand out from the rest of the class; I might have missed her among the blonde curls and ginger ponytails. She handed me her assignment and I weighed it between my fingers, the paper thick and buttery. I looked a second time at the girl standing in front of me and noticed she was pretty. Pixie-faced, with a short dark helmet of hair that made her eyes seem bigger than they were. By exam time I was regularly helping her zip up her linen tunic, her perfume still appealing then; not quite yet the scent of a familiar but uninteresting room.

It was her exploration of form that kept me entranced till just after her graduation. A double major, arts and technology. She brought a different world with her to the page, a curious experimentation. Tricks, I called them, but she would not be dissuaded from her experiments in narrative. And even before she won the award for the interactive narrative, I had to admit that some of them were quite good.

I hold the memory stick up to my nose as if I might smell her fingers on it. Nothing. Plastic, a petrochemical base note. There is a piece of characteristically heavy paper in the envelope—*Thanks for this*—and on the flipside—*I value your feedback.*

There is a suit to go with it. A skin. That's what they call them. I hold the thing up, weighing it, turning it. It is just like a skin that someone might have shed, a whole person degloved, rubbery, flesh coloured, damply cold.

I pour a glass and sit by the laptop. Liv's email has instructions. This is a memoir. Ten years in the making. *First Person Present Tense.* I'd like to thank you for the lessons you taught me. Voice is everything—you were right.

I sip and tap the memory stick on the kitchen counter. 'Bach,' I say and the computer anticipates my track choice: cello suites. I lean back and shut my eyes and Plain Jane hovers in my memory, pushing back her luxurious tresses. Liv was interesting, smart, a handful, but Jane, now Jane…

I tap my finger on the side of the glass. Even with Bach to calm me I can't settle. How could this be the future of memoir? How could a memory stick and a synthetic suit replace Nin and Levi and Thoreau? I push the glass aside, barely touched. Suiting up is quite a process. At this time in the evening I would rather be putting on my tracksuit pants. It feels too intimate, the fabric, a little like neoprene but sheerer, softer against naked skin, the little tube-shaped pouch for the penis. It feels almost pornographic to slip myself inside it. I suppose there is a different model for the ladies but I can't imagine how the crotch would be configured. I think of Plain Jane easing her suit on, rolling the tight fabric up her smooth leg, and I appreciate how the material adjusts for all the slight changes that might occur in the course of a viewing session.

They use these suits for porn. Of course. Pornography is the driver for most innovation. If it weren't for the needs of men we would never have shot off into space.

I press the sliver of plastic into the slot in the machine. I slip the headpiece into place and my eyes adjust to the optical limits. A grey line begins to turn blue, the words pairing suit above it.

First Person Present Tense.

Prologue.

Perhaps the title is a little obvious. I'll tell her this. Why is it impossible to make notes when you are in this skin? *Title*, I squeeze my eyes shut to commit the note to memory. *Tell her to change the title.* Then it begins.

I am momentarily confused. I am watching myself. I recognise the university, a lecture theatre, probably in L Block although I have never seen it from this angle. I am sitting in an audience of students. I can feel the press of the seat back, the shift of the swivelling lap table across my knees. I never realised how hard these seats are. I never knew how constricted you can feel when the tabletop is swung into place. I look down at the table and there is my laptop. No. Not my laptop. This is a more modern laptop. Mine has travelled with me for ten years—upgrades, add-ons—heavy and silver and uncomfortable. This one is lighter and sleeker. I remember it. This is Liv's laptop that she replaced with a more powerful model when she graduated. These are Liv's tight black jeans constricting my hips. Liv's high heels slipped onto my feet. The left one tapping against the seat in front of me, her. On Liv's laptop screen there is a flashing red word. Remembering. Remembering. I am pacing back and forth in front of myself, no, in front of Liv.

'Voice.'

Oh god, the shirt. Do I really look that chubby in it? Do I even own that shirt anymore? Purple check, the warping across the protrusion of my stomach. I try to suck my gut in but I can't and needn't. I am slim as a girl. I am a girl. I am Liv.

I can't breathe. I fumble for the headpiece, the mask, whatever it is called in this mess of silicon and circuitry. I snap it off and take deep breaths. Parallel lines sit in the middle of my laptop screen, my heavy old silver computer. The universal symbol for a paused feed. It is strange to be back here in my own body. I catch a glimpse of my face reflected in the dull blue of the screen. I am six years older now. That plump version of myself must have been one of the first times we met. I didn't even remember her name back then. She was one of the many faceless students. I have a whole new batch of them now and each new crop is exactly the same as the last.

I take a big swallow of wine. I feel myself returning, occupying my body once more. A draft licks at my cheek. I have left a window open somewhere.

Was I really that old even then? I am tempted to get up, go to a mirror, find myself again. Of course it is just a trick of perspective or technology: a bad lens, a dodgy angle. I know what I look like.

Below the pause symbol there is a line and the word Contents. I click on the word and there are chapter numbers, Prologue, Chapter 1, Chapter 2 all the way to Chapter 34 and then an epilogue. I hover the arrow over the first chapter and click. The cursor flashes, waiting for me to put the headpiece back on. I take deep breaths as if I were about to plunge into icy water. Then, when my head is spinning from hyperventilation, I slip the mask back onto my head.

Again, a moment of disorientation. It is as if I have been swallowed whole by a creature barely larger than myself, a croc or a shark. My muscles tense to cut my way out, emerge like Jonah, triumphant and covered in ambergris. But the panic settles. The new skin eases snug against my own, becomes my own, its eyes my eyes, the mechanical iris making its adjustments. Pairing suit. The new world becoming clear, clearer than the old, real world. Everything leaps crisply into focus. A room, the smell of it, at once familiar and yet unfamiliar. I sniff. That scent, cloves, cut grass and dust. An old-book scent and the reek of unwashed sheets. It smells like...my own bedroom, and yet different. Heightened. I blink and take an unbalanced step into the room. A moment of dizziness, then I reach out and touch the wall. My own bedroom wall. It is solid. I am home. But I'm not, I'm not in my bedroom. I struggle against this new overlap of reality. I know I am sitting in the kitchen, plugged in to Liv's program, clad in a suit, a second skin. I try to turn, to walk back to where I know I am sitting, but nothing happens. I have no agency in this story. I run my fingers without volition—my fingers are run—over the flock wallpaper. I look down at the piles of books lining the wall. The titles leap into focus as I stare: Knausgaard, Atwood, Orwell, Yuknavitch...Nin, although I know the Nin is no longer there. I lent that book to a student, the one who superseded Liv. Slimmer waist, longer hair, bigger tits. But here is the book, returned to its rightful place in the pile at my feet. I pick up the Yuknavitch, *The Chronology of Water,* and turn it in my hands. I am wearing nail polish. Green on the right hand and on the left a darker green, almost brown, a shimmering like the carapace of a beetle. I vaguely remember knowing a girl who did this, two different colours at once, who was it?

'You can borrow that. You'd like it.' It is my voice, close to my ear. Someone behind me. I am behind me. 'You've read C. A. Elphick?' I can feel myself nodding. It is unsettling to nod without willing myself to nod, to be a passive participant in my own actions. I struggle to shake my head, but no. I have to sit in this body and be moved like a puppet. Nod, nod, nod.

'Well, she owes a lot to Yuknavitch. *Writing the Silence* is like a little cousin to that book.'

I am putting the book back on the pile when a hand reaches out to still mine. Fingers touch, interlink. The book becomes an excuse for hand-holding, a finger gently stroking mine, and I am suddenly aroused. I turn my head and there is a tall man behind me. Just like with my bedroom, he is familiar, someone I have known. He reminds me of my father, same barrel chest, same grey and thinning hair. He leans closer. A twitch deep inside me like the slow rise of a penis, only one that is buried in the pit of my belly. The penis thickens and throbs as the man leans close and presses his mouth against mine and forces my lips rudely open with his tongue and stabs at my upper palate, snailing over the back of my teeth. The pulse in my belly might be lust or fear and it is too big, it is tearing a hole inside me. I am paused at the beginning of a sprint; my heart is too fast. I can't breathe.

When the man pulls away there is blood on his lip, and I realise that it must be my blood, my lip split in the violence of that kiss.

But no. Not blood. Lipstick. It is my lipstick smeared onto his mouth. I can see a pulse beating at the base of his neck. I can see his trousers pulling tight at his crotch. I press the Yuknavitch to my chest. My chest. The breasts soft and warm under my fingers. A confusion of desire. I try to cup them, my breasts, but my hands will not let go of the cool chaste cover of the book.

He cups them for me. He reaches out and shapes his hands around my breasts and pushes the hard lump in his crotch against me and tilts his head down, smiling. And I know him. I recognise him from the other world, the real world. It is me of course, this man. In the other world I see him smiling at me in the mirror, catch glimpses of him as I walk past shop windows, see him in photographs.

Me. Of course it is me.

And I am her. I am Liv. And this is my room and it is his room and he, I, put my hand up her, my, skirt. I push the cotton aside with his finger and it catches on the pubic hair, which stings sharply and his finger wriggling inside me is like sandpaper and I am trying not to wince as he finally gets the finger—sharp ragged nail—into the complication of folds and touches the very edge of her void. The horror and the beauty of it. The feeling of a slick damp finger, less pain, more pleasure in it now as he fingers me. I finger her. I remember fingering her that first time, standing in my bedroom, I am the subject of this probing, not quite enjoying it, not really sure if I should push his hand away.

I push his hand away and my lips are slick with my anxious desire and I smell him, musky, strong, predatory, and he raises his finger to his face and sniffs it, touches it to his lips, wetting them, and there is a rush of saliva—not saliva, not come, but a wet warm spurt nonetheless and it dampens my underwear.

I did that. I am doing it. It is me. I slip my finger into my mouth and I hold her hips, not her, my hips with the sharp, bruising fingers of his other hand. He holds me so hard that any pleasure dissipates as he pushes that spit-wet finger inside me and rams it all the way up. One, two, three times in quick succession. And it hurts. This little pistoning finger that I know to be the Auslan gesture for *fucking.* A furious triple *fuck you.*

And I remember what is to come and I am struggling to forget just as I am struggling against his rough clamp of a fist. And I hear her in memory, an echo, as I say, '*No.*'

And I say, 'Stop,' or is it my memory of her?

No. And Stop.

And it stops.

I am sitting on a chair in my kitchen and I am breathing hard in the suffocation of the mask. The parallel pause lines glow in the middle distance. The story has stopped. I must have spoken aloud. The narrative responded to my words.

I snap the headpiece off and the world comes back to me. My thick thighs, my masculine waist, my cock standing hard, stiff against the fabric. I unzip the suit and peel it off. The rancid smell of anxious sweat wafts from my sticky skin. I make my way to the bedroom. My bedroom. Here. In my house. My piles of books. The Yuknavitch there where it has always been in a pile of memoirs and biography.

I touch the wall. My fingers stroke the flock wallpaper. I have never really thought about the wallpaper before. I press the palm of my hand onto it and feel a finger sandpapering its way inside me. The smell of my sweat, her cunt. The taste of her, first taste that time right here where I am standing. I take hold of my cock, slipping my fist down over it. Sandpaper-dry fist. But I pump it anyway, remembering the day as it happened. Remembering the next thing. The sharp surprise of her hymen. How excited I was by the discovery of her virginity.

I spit on my hand and take my cock again, remembering. Not quite remembering. All I can grab hold of is the memory of pushing, hard, trying to break it. Knowing I was the first and swelling up with that knowledge. A conquistador, an astronaut planting his flag. Splitting the cunt of her wide open and seeding her virgin field. All the old clichés.

I rub myself hard. I am older now. I was so hard pushing myself against her. She was collecting it all. I'm not sure how, was there some device, some secret camera? How do the kids do that stuff anyway? First-person video games or whatever they call it now.

But this isn't a game, this is something else. Not a camera. She was naked. I remember or almost remember that first time with her. Was she naked? Did I let her leave some part of her clothing on? I rub, but my cock is deflating. I am squeezing the air out of that particular balloon. Did I let her keep her clothes on?

It is the doubt that bothers me. The gaps in memory. And now with the limp curl of my penis soft against the palm of my hand I feel my anger flushing my skin.

She recorded me without permission. I will sue her. This is my reputation here. If this thing got out, this file, this game, the first-person shooter or whatever high-tech thing. This skewed version of things. If this got out? If my students saw this…

My cock leaps at the injustice of it. A little angry stab and I squeeze it again, once, twice, three times, remembering that first finger-fuck. That sweet fresh sap filling my nose. That tight first-fingered cunt hole. I remember she was a virgin, but I didn't know that then. Popping the cherry they call it, because of the blood. No blood marring the first taste of her.

My mouth waters, my cock swells anew but I rub without coming. Rubbing and rubbing, my cheek pressed against the flock wallpaper, my cock aimed towards Lidia Yuknavitch. Liv is a bitch, a bitch with a camera hidden somewhere.

Bitch. Rub. Bitch. Rub.

I let go of my penis, panting, sweating. I stomp back towards the kitchen. The suit is difficult to drag on. My hair catches; pulls. I remember the tug of my pubic hair, his (my) finger in my pants. I grunt into the suit and zip it up, gentling the fabric up to cover my penis, now fully erect.

There is that momentary dislocation as I put the mask on. A moment of suffocation. The beat of her heart is faster than mine. I can feel the disconnect, a syncopation, that rise of the ocean and the sudden plummet but then my heart makes pace with hers and we are one. I am up against the flock wallpaper. I can feel it softly scratching against the cheeks of my arse.

He is too heavy against my chest. The thud of his belt on my pubis is sharp and unpleasant. I struggle away but it is persistent like a dentist's drill. This dull metal tapping against bone. His hands grab at my arse, push up, settle me onto his body. My knees spread wide, the lips of my vulva swollen and sensitive. I can feel them chafing. This is what it feels like? I shake my head, but of course I am not shaking my head in this moment within moments. I feel fear. Is it my fear? My real and present fear? Or is it her fear, has this program somehow plugged me into a recorded memory of fear? How do you do that, I wonder as he lurches across to the unmade bed with me, held too high and clutched too tight. How do you record a sensation of fear? Is it the heart rate communicated through the tiny receptors in the rubber? Is it a change of temperature, a tightening of the second skin?

How is this story 'written'? And what part of it is authored? What percentage comes from the reader? Am I afraid now because I have never experienced 'the lips of my vulva' before? Am I scared of the possibility of a vagina, of my body embracing this magician's trick without missing a single beat? Or was she, Liv, frightened six years ago when I picked her up and threw her down onto the plump of my bed?

I am shaking my head now, or she is, as he climbs between my spread knees and pins me with his sheer bulk. And I am shivering a little, clamping all those unfamiliar girl parts shut.

This must be my fear, my masculine self responding to the idea of penetration. I struggle for distance from the feel of his hands on my knickers as he struggles them down. Part of me remembers how it really was. She was warm and welcoming beneath me. She was wet and ready for me, urging me on. Wasn't she?

I shake my head but I remain silent as he wrenches the tangle of underwear off one of my trembling feet. He lifts his hips off me for a moment and I hear the sound of a zipper. His face is on my face, his closed eyes, the wrinkles beside his nose, a close-up of open pores. His tongue missing my mouth entirely, a wet line across my cheek until he finds his target and the tongue darts hard between my lips.

Hard between my lips.

Is this how it feels, the slip of cock missing its mark? He shifts and my knee is pushed wider from the weight of him and the buckle of his belt cuts at the flesh of my thigh. He thrusts again and there is no way that thing is going in me. It couldn't. I try to wriggle my hips away, I twist but his hand is down there, I can feel his fingers hooking into the meat of me. Yes. I am wet. He slips on juices and fumbles. Can a woman be wet when she is afraid? I would never have expected this physical contradiction. There is lubrication all around the area and it is only this that allows his finger to slip past my tight clenched lips. He pauses. I wriggle, but he presses down to hold me still. His finger pokes away down there. He is feeling the surface of my hymen, exploring it, plucking it like a string on a guitar, playing a hiss of air out of me, a grunt escaping around the slug tongue.

His fingers retreat and he is breathing heavily onto my cheek, into my hair. I have excited him, or the barriers of my body have. My mouth is free and I speak for the first time since hitting the bed.

'I...I'm not sure...'

But the words are interrupted by a punch. It feels like a punch although I'm not sure if you can call a cock barrelling towards a cunt a punch exactly. A pounding is the right expression as the thwack of it speeds up, bruising the sticky lips, numbing them with thump after thump and then a sharp pain, a cutting, and I cry out. And he stops. He is lodged a little in me. Part of him finally settled inside my flesh.

He pauses. We pant. The pain is less sharp. I can bear it. I suppose I am losing, have lost my virginity. I wasn't ready, but it is done.

Hang on, are these my thoughts? Her thoughts? I try to

surface, slide back down to the place where I am shaking but I let relief flood through me because it is over and I have survived.

Then he lifts his hips and I feel the cock sliding out of me and just before it loses contact with the sting of my flesh it slams down once more and I have never felt pain like this. I whimper uncontrollably and maybe the sob of pain is like a sob of pleasure because he is encouraged by it. He lifts and drops and there is more of it inside me. A big fist of gristle lodged in my skin. Lift and drop, lift and drop further. I grit my teeth at each new humiliation. Then he picks his weight off my chest and props himself up and looks down at what must be the bloodied pulp of my sex and he puts his hand down there. I can feel him measuring his own girth.

Then the fucking starts, fast pumping thrusts as I lie spread and bleeding and growing mercifully numb beneath him. He fucks and there are words on his lips and some of them slip out in counterpoint to his pumping.

'...right...up...up...fu...tight...first fuck...first...'

And then his eyes become wide and white, the irises disappear completely and he stretches his lips into a grin before grunting the words 'There you go', and rocking, jerking, stopping, jerking and falling with a grunt onto my face, chest hair in my mouth. Another sharp twitch into me and a stinging like alcohol poured on an open wound.

The only sound from me is a sharp, pained hiss.

'That was fucking wonderful,' he says, slipping his hand down again and checking that he is still lodged there. He bounces his soft cock in and out a few times, paddling in the shallows. Then he pushes a kiss into my cheek and looks down at my pale face and says it:

'You're a woman now.' He really does. Another pressing of the lips. 'Did you come?'

I close my eyes and in the darkness words, my voice, her voice in my head. They are clear and certain. This is what you would call a voiceover. My voiceover. But no. I shake her off with difficulty. I struggle to remember myself within her.

The voice says: And in this way it begins.

There is come in the suit. I don't know how it happened, even now, thinking back on the scene I am becoming aroused again. It is horrifying. How could so much pain and fear make me come? Make the sticky relief of my penis start to get hard again?

The scene lacked all the things I usually need to push me to orgasm. The sight of a girl, particularly the tits. Where were her tits in all of this? He, I, didn't suck one tit into my mouth in the whole experience. That can't be possible. I don't remember it like that at all, but to be honest I don't remember much about it except that first realisation that she was a virgin and how my knees trembled when I knew I was about to help her be rid of that childlike state. I do remember needing to wash the sheets twice, soaking them in a bucket of bleach between washes. I almost remember it as a sweet, tender moment between us. I almost remember it.

I lie now, naked on the bed and my cock standing and I

lather it with lube from the bedside table and although it is hard I can barely feel it in my fist. Instead I feel the push of a cock. I feel cunt. I feel sharp pain. I feel ill. Bile rising from my gut. Come rising from my balls. I spasm, shooting a second time. I turn my head and vomit. It sprays, yellow as jaundice across the sheets. I roll onto my knees and my body is racked with the purging spasms as my cock still pumps the last of its bitter seed onto the sheets.

I stand up, dizzy. Seasick. She has poisoned me. Bitch, I think, but without heat. If that was really how it was, that first time with Liv...

I rip the sheets from the bed and throw them in the bathtub. I turn the shower on above them and fall back to sit on the toilet.

If that was real, then I am implicated in it.

It felt real. I felt what Liv might have felt. Or was it some trick? Surely what I have just experienced was like falling into someone's unreliable memoir. A lie. A very cleverly drawn one, but a lie nonetheless.

I wash the come out of the suit. There is a special protective coating on the inside, thicker around the crotch area. Pornography drives innovation. I suppose it must be so.

I fall pale and shaking onto the fresh sheets. I will have to rewrite the dossier. This more than anything bothers me. The fact that my course outline for Memoir 104 will have to be updated. Not now, but sometime soon. If this is a future for narrative, I will have to be at the forefront of teaching it. I cross my arms over my breasts, only I have no breasts. I try to remember the skin that I am in. I have 'read' three chapters. If it wasn't for the 8 a.m. lecture I would have finished the whole thing, staying up to experience my own life retold to me, by her but in my skin—or no, in her skin. I have never felt so unsettled. Tomorrow's lecture will cover the rise of the sexual memoir, from the pseudonymous memoirs of female prostitutes (written by men) to modern accounts of web affairs, second-life sex, and last year's bestseller, *Recollections of a Proxy Sexxer.* All of it superseded now. Soon the page will not be the place for it. I will have to look more closely at the lecture on ethics in light of this new thing, this unrecognisable version of myself.

I close my eyes and roll over onto the fat of the pillow and remember the softness of the skin I have been inhabiting. I could sue. Surely defamation laws cover this. I wonder if she could mask my identity somehow, some CGI technique, another body over my skin. Even then I would not be protected. Some people knew about us, our affair. Sometimes she would step out of my car wearing one of my shirts, her own shirt lying in my washing basket stained by my jism. Sometimes she sat in my class, her eyes averted but with all eyes on her. They knew. They would know. I could sue. But then I would have to admit it was me who held her down and forced myself upon her, who humiliated her.

I have lived through a chapter where I critique her essay in front of the class, sneering at the lack of analysis, at the gush of subjectivity. Then at home, making up for it with sex that I assumed was mutually pleasurable. I have struggled to contain my tears while lying powerless beneath the bulk of my own body, faking an orgasm just to get my weight off my own chest. How could I stand up in court and say, *Yes, that was me. That was all me, but despite what you have seen, ladies and gentlemen of the jury, it wasn't like that at all.* Not at all. Honestly. If you could see inside my head you would have a different story. As the officers of the court approach: *No. Please. I am innocent.* And they take me by the arm, one on each side. *No honestly, it isn't like that. She has remembered it all wrong.* And they half-drag, half-carry me down the aisle and I catch my shin on a pew and I wake up.

I have slept. I groan and ease my legs out of bed, dropping them over and onto the floor. My head throbs. I stumble into the bathroom. The dirty sheets are still bundled in the bottom of the bath. I let the cold water run through them, rinsing away the smell of vomit and the memory of a bad night. When they are clean enough I bundle them into the washing machine and watch the slow sudsy spin begin. I step under the shower. I will be similarly cleansed. I can feel the water outlining my body for me. I am me. I am in this body. I am surrounded by water. I am the person I always thought I was, not her vision of me.

As I rub myself dry with the bath sheet I become myself.

They are watching me. I am aware of them now. All eyes on me and I see myself here, my threadbare cardigan over a T-shirt with a comic panel on the front. Zombies approaching a car. The hero standing on top of the car with a cricket bat. I am probably too old now for a novelty T-shirt. I pull the cardigan close around my chest and fumble the buttons closed. Maybe I should start working out. It would be good for my health to start some physical activity. I am fatter in the stomach than I would like to be.

Jane is looking at me. Plain Jane, who is so far from plain. I smile in her direction. I feel a sudden need to accelerate my habitual leisurely seduction. I need her to think of me in a different way. I need her eyes, glancing approvingly at my belly, my solid hips, my chest. I need her to give me back my cock, which used always to be so present. It has become difficult to imagine myself without a vulva, and I need to address this as soon as possible. I need Plain Jane to smile back at me, to see me as a man.

She smiles. I feel my feet planted more firmly on the floor. I open my laptop. A flutter of panic. I track my cursor to the finder, search for the file in case it has embedded itself there, but I ejected the slim memory stick before I left. It is carefully tucked away in the envelope it came in. Her address on the back. Evidence.

'Today,' I say to the class, but I am really speaking to one person. I keep coming back to her, locking my gaze to hers. 'Today we will discuss how a writer can seduce a reader.' The predicted swell of laughter from the group. They are still young. This doesn't change. In all my years of teaching, every first-year group will laugh in embarrassment when the subject of sex is even vaguely referenced. 'As a writer,' I say, 'you are in complete control of the story. You have the reader in your hands. And as with any seduction, it is up to you to...land the fish, shall we say. Tickle it out of the water. Like a trout. Have you heard of trout tickling?' Lots of heads shaking. 'Well, look that up some time. The reader is like the fish and you just need to get your hands under there. A little tickle to reassure them. Then you follow up quick smart and land them. Seduction. Look that one up, too, while you are at it. It is an art, a craft. You have to craft your story so that it seduces the reader.'

She doesn't take her eyes off me. It won't be hard to get her. She has read my novel, or she should have. It was required reading for last semester's fiction subject. She has read it and therefore half my work has been done for me. She has been tickled. My hands are already hovering under her. All that I need do now is to lift her and flip her onto the shore.

Jane seems nervous. She holds her satchel in front of her, shielding her crotch. I step aside, holding the door open. She has to push past me to get inside and her skin presses against my shirt. I smell her perfume, sweet and unapologetically feminine.

My own house feels unfamiliar. I dump my briefcase on the table where I always put it. I shrug my jumper off onto the back of the lounge. I open the fridge, my fridge, and pull out the wine, my wine, but I am seeing all of it through a distorted lens. Each action familiar and yet equally unfamiliar.

'You have so many books.' She says this as if she is

surprised that a lecturer in literature might read books. She touches a row of them with her delicate fingers, each one tipped with a pale shell pink. I imagine her fingers spreading those similarly coloured lips. Her nails seem to promise me the pink of her sex. I take her hand and wrap those cuntish fingers around a glass of sauvignon blanc. This is a perfect beginning.

She is here to borrow *Speak Memory* by Nabokov but of course we both know that isn't the reason we are here. She wouldn't like the book anyway. I glance down at her tanned and hairless legs, the elegant red high heels that she slips off one by one, easing her feet into the long pile of the carpet as if it were unmowed lawn. She is like an old-fashioned girl from seventies soft porn. She is all warm limbs and Vaseline lens.

She plumps herself down on the couch and crosses her legs and her skirt kicks up. She manages to seem shy and flirty all at once. This would be the signal to pounce as she arranges herself in front of me. She glances up at me, stretching her neck as if to offer her throat. I ease myself onto the couch beside her and I could so easily lean forward, press my lips onto her skin. This would restore me to myself. I take a long sip of my wine. I lean forward, looming over her.

Looming.

I see this with a strange sense of deja vu: I have been here before, only I was the one being loomed at. I lean towards her and she stretches her chin up and out and I see myself leaning down to breathe on my neck. I am displaced. I am at once both the hunter and hunted. Too late to waver now, my lips are so close to that pale throat, the pearly fingertips reaching up to cup the stubble on my cheek. I bury my face in skin. I breathe in flowers, flesh petals it seems, with my eyes closed and the gentle brush of her against my mouth. She is floral. Her face is a bouquet. I am lurching between one perspective and the next, her face, mine.

I pull back, dizzy. I take deep breaths. I try to be still within myself but I can't seem to find my equilibrium.

I close my eyes. My skin feels too naked on my body. I am vulnerable. It takes me a moment to realise that what I am missing is that other skin, that rubber-like material that heightens as it curates my bodily relationship with the world. My skin on her skin is just too intimate and yet even my leg pressed against hers feels like it is a long way away from her body. And something else, as she shifts, puts her hands up to the front of her summer frock, undoes one button after another, even with the lace of a bra poking up above the pastel-coloured cotton, all this feels like an interruption. These are not the people in the story of my life. This man I am inhabiting, this woman I am about to find my way into, these are mere distractions. Even the possibility of sex with this girl feels like an irritation.

The suit is where I left it, drying on a rack in the bathroom. It is the thought of it that stirs me now. I feel myself beginning to become firm. I kiss her, imagining the tight grasp of the fabric on my calves. The suit is mine to wear, the story is mine to inhabit. Hard now, I push myself onto this girl. I knew her name but now I have forced it out of the way. She is just some warm thing under me as I fumble with her knickers, unzip, unbuckle. I feel the shape of my penis and it feels like the first time in a long while. The warm wet clutch of her cunt gives me length and breadth again. I measure the whole length of myself in a single thrust. Male again. I withdraw and lose my sense of it as I lose connection with her body. I thrust in again and my cock is returned to me, three-dimensional, whole. I punch it into her, swelling a little each time, floating up into my sense of self, but at what seems to be maximum altitude I begin to plummet. I fall into—no, become—a chasm. I open to a cold, hard disappointment. I am my cock and yet I am also the disappointment of flesh, losing all hope of pleasure, thrust by agonising thrust.

I feel the infusion of loneliness that will be numbing her thighs. Each awkward forward motion pushing her further away from me. I know her eagerness to please and also the glimmer of an understanding swelling deep in her belly. This old man will be no different from any of the young men. This old man, expert in narrative structure, is inexpert in the business of sex. This man, me, I am slightly unclean, unskilled, good for nothing when I step out of a lecture theatre and ease into a willing young girl.

I am deflating. My cock bends painfully at the next thrust. I lift it out of her, letting the lips of her cunt suck at the sudden cold rush of air. I open my eyes. The nausea rises up to meet me and I pull away, flinging myself to the far side of the couch. Her dress is pulled high, her knees parted. I can see the red pucker of her vulva pursed at the edge of her knickers. The cotton slips back, almost hides her slit from my gaze. Her cheeks are flushed. Her eyes are locked onto the shrivelled worm of my penis, glistening wet and hanging sadly from my open fly.

I hold my hand to my mouth, my stomach clamps down on itself. I feel a hot rush in my throat and swallow it down quickly, and when I am safe from the attacks of my own body I look back at her. Jane. I remember now. Plain Jane with the porcelain inner thighs and the perfectly bald shell-pink lip still poking out the side of her damp underwear and her pink lipstick kissing the rim of her wine glass, abandoned hurriedly on the side table.

'Get up,' I tell her. I can see that she is confused. 'Get up,' I say again, and, 'Go away.'

She blinks, and very slowly moves her pinked fingers to her crotch. She plucks the elastic from its lodging and smooths the skirt of the dress over her knees.

'Done with me?' she asks. And then, with her lip curled up a little, 'Doctor Greenwald?'

I am thirsty. I reach for my glass and sip but wine is not what I am hoping for. I need some water.

'It would seem so,' I tell her.

She finds her shoes and her bag and then she opens the fridge door and plucks the bottle of wine off the shelf and carries it with her to the door.

'Thanks for the drink.' She holds the bottle up to make sure I have seen it.

I shrug. She hates me. If I had continued on with it, met her tomorrow and the next day and the next, then she would have hated me more. As much as Liv hated me. Hates me. Hates me, in the present tense. I put my cock away and zip up. The memory stick is where I left it last night.

Memory stick. That is exactly what it is. I pick her memory up and turn it between my fingers. Each scene plays out in real time but there are breaks, cracks in her recollection. The recreation of her history skips over the boring bits or the bits she has forgotten. Last night I immersed myself in three weeks of trysts and emerged from it before the next day arrived. I wonder how long it will take to trudge through the three long years of our time together.

Will she include the time we borrowed a car from her mother? The quick duck to the hills? Would a reader have to suffer through each of the three Christmases, with their respective aggressions and humiliations?

I walk quickly to the bathroom. I am out of my clothes and pulling the suit on before I have time to rethink. Just to check, I tell myself, just to know what she has included and what she has left out. I step inside the skin and zip it up and I might as well have shrugged her body around my own shoulders. I can even smell her on me, an earthy musk. I breathe it in, knowing that it is an illusion. I sit at the same table. My laptop. Her memory stick.

I pull the mask over my head.

*

The phone is ringing. I try to reach into my handbag for it but I can't and so it must be a phone in that other place. I am sitting at a cafe. There is a damp tissue in my hand. I am eating a slice of cheesecake to wash the taste of the woman off my lips. I don't hate her. She is just another of his students, but she is prettier than I am. Her breasts are bigger. She is more skilled at taking him in her mouth. I dutifully let him push my head down between her legs and pretended to like it. I pretended to like what he wanted. I press the tissue to my eyes but they are dry now. He didn't kiss me once. Her face was slick with his spit and yet he didn't kiss me once. I touch the tissue to my lips. The phone rings. I try to purse my lips angrily but I can't feel any anger. There is just the terrible wrenching sadness, and the slack frown.

But the phone.

My fingers are numb. It is almost impossible to fumble the mask off my head. The parallel pause lines leap into view. They are like a slap in my face. I am falling backward, but no, not me, the world is slipping away and I am still upright. I flex my fingers till the circulation returns to them. I have been clutching the edge of the table so hard my fingers feel bruised.

My phone is ringing. It is in the pocket of my jacket, which is still lying crumpled on the lounge chair. I look at it lying there and it is as if the jacket is a person, someone I abandoned, mewing like a kitten, lost, lonely. Jane. I am equating my jacket with Jane and remembering her feels terrible. I am filled with a rush of self-loathing and, worse, I am filled with a sense of my physicality. I was the man who pushed Liv's head down on Lee's crotch. I was the man who pulled myself and aimed it at her mouth, spilling across Lee's clitoris as she licked it. I was that man. It makes me want to crawl back into the suit just to escape the fact of my history.

I glance to the window. The sun is just beginning to set. I have only been in the suit for a few hours but it feels like weeks.

I push up to standing, sway. I have lost my balance and I sit down again. The phone stops ringing. I hear a last isolated beep telling me I have a message.

I stand again, with more success this time, using the table to support my weight. I am ravenously hungry, and so thirsty I could drink a gallon of water. I stumble into the kitchen and stand at the tap pouring glass after glass. The phone rings again but now I need to urinate. My bladder feels swollen, ready to burst. I unzip the suit and it is too late to run to the toilet. I grab a plastic mixing bowl and sink into the relief of pissing.

I notice that the suit is sticky at the crotch. I have come again. Several times, by the look of it. It must have been in that scene, I remember it now as I shake off the last drops and tip the bowl into the sink. A stink of urine fugs up into my face. That scene where I crept out of his bed—my bed—and locked myself in the bathroom and put one finger into myself and brushed the index finger of my other hand up and down across my clitoris until the lips of my vulva began to pulse, sucking at my finger. My first orgasm as a woman. Or her first orgasm with me, but not with me.

I trot over to my jacket and fumble for my phone.

'Caspar?'

It takes me a minute to recognise the voice of Arthur, acting head of school.

'Yes?'

'Thank goodness. You're alive.'

'I am.'

'Where were you? Why didn't you call in?'

'Call?' I move over to the window, lift one of the venetians. The sun is just beginning to set. It can't be later than six o'clock.

'Lucy covered your class but we were worried.'

'Oh,' I say and check the face of my phone. Thursday. Thursday night, 5:16 p.m. What happened to the rest of Wednesday? What happened to a whole new morning and a day? Could I have been sitting in that chair the whole time? My back aches and I stretch it out, leaning forward and resting my forehead on the sill.

'I think I've come down with something nasty.'

'We thought so.'

'I seem to have...slept all day.'

'No problem. Take your time. Just checking you're okay.'

I pause. I am not really sure if I am okay.

'I might take tomorrow off.'

'Good idea. We'll see you Monday. Go to the doctor.'

I nod but I'm not sure if a doctor can cure what I have.

I look at my phone. Scroll through the contact list. I find

her name. Liv. Phone number, email and address. I wonder if she is okay now. It has been years, but is she okay? I never once thought to wonder what her life has been like. She was in it, and then she was gone. I sent her away. She rang, kept ringing, but I just let it go to message. I thought it would be easier for her, for the breakup. Or did I? Did I think that? Or did I just not want to think at all?

There was that girl with the really long hair. Hair to her thighs. Took her hours to caress it all with a straightener. She was already in the picture before I kicked Liv out. It was that strand of hair, that single fine thread, so long when I picked it out of the drain. Liv had to go before there were more hairs, in the sheets, swept under the kitchen bench, wrapped loosely around my balls. That's why I kicked her out. It was to save her from knowing or to save me from the aftermath of her knowing.

I lie back on the couch, exhausted. I am still hungry. I flick through my phone and call the number for the pizza place down the road. I order extra garlic bread, a packet of M&M's. I could eat two pizzas but I just order the one.

I lie with the phone to my chest. Liv. I wonder what happened to Liv. I should get out of the suit but it is so comfortable now, warm and supple. I zip it up and hug my arms around the rubber shell. I slip the mask back over my face and click into the chapter menu. I am halfway through. Almost exactly. This is the mid-point in our story. I am tempted to play this out, just to the end of the scene, but I know I will become lost in it. My stomach groans. I haven't eaten in almost twenty-four hours. I need a coffee.

I peel the suit off and head back to the kitchen. I pour bleach into the sink and run the tap. The acid tang of urine is replaced by the alkaline slap of bleach. I throw the bowl straight into the recycling bin.

While the coffee is brewing I snack on bocconcini from the plastic container. I eat a handful of olives and the oil runs down to my elbow. I wash my hands in dishwashing liquid. I am exhausted, and feverish, as if I really do have the flu. I slip my bathrobe on and sip coffee till the pizza arrives. The young man glances down at the rubber leggings poking out from beneath my robe but says nothing. He takes the tip I offer him and leaves quietly. Maybe he thought he'd interrupted me in the middle of some fetish game.

Did he? I am certainly aroused when I lie back on the couch and pull the mask back onto my face. I am about to press play but then I roll over and wake up and although I am still in the suit I have not experienced anything but the cold dark emptiness of the universe and me plummeting through it.

I would shower but that would take effort. I would have to get out of the suit. Taking the suit off at this point feels like it might hurt. Even when I unzip to take a piss it feels as if I am cutting myself open with a blade. I hold my stomach with one hand in case my bowels fall out through the gap in the suit. I zip up with no mishaps. And re-skinned I set the table with a picnic lunch, grazing on bread and cheese as I do it. I must eat. I must stop and eat and drink and defecate. I have a body and no matter how odd it feels to be inside my own body, it will need some sustenance or it will not be strong enough to finish what I have begun here.

I am still swallowing a mouthful of coffee and a slice of ham when I press play. My teeth are chewing and I am swallowing and it is a nice segue because I am eating a toasted sandwich in the narrative, sucking up thick mucus along with tears each time I sniff loudly. I have been crying. This is real. This sucking in of air, the salt on the back of my palate. This is real. I have a vague distasteful memory of ordering pizza. It feels like that might have been a long time ago, or perhaps it is just a story someone told me, like when your mother tells you about that time you fell off the swing and needed stitches. The brief, distasteful tussle with Plain Jane is just a terrible story I have been told, a cautionary tale.

The waiter brings me a box of tissues with a little flower on top of it. A paper daisy. Small kindnesses. It makes me weep out loud. I turn to thank him but he is gone. I pull six tissues from the box and blow my nose into each of them till I am surrounded by soggy wads. When I can breathe more easily I put the daisy behind my ear. I am sure my eyes are puffy and my face is beetroot red but this small thing, a flower, makes me feel a little bit human again. Perhaps even attractive. Not attractive like that other girl, not all long legs and pillowy breasts and glossy hair, but someone a waiter might notice. Someone who might deserve a small floral tribute.

*

I think I have lost weight. I look at myself in the fogged mirror. My body, my now unfamiliar hips, legs, shoulders. Showers are certainly quicker in this body. I don't need to blow-dry then style my hair. I don't need to paint my face with base then powder then eyeliner then, then, then, then. I towel myself dry and I slip a robe over my shoulders. I should wash the suit properly, there are instructions on the lid of the box. There is a special disinfectant that the manufacturer provides. I am almost at the end of it now. The breakup is inevitable. Maybe there will be one more twist, a happily-ever-after ending plucked from a hope rather than a memory.

In the narrative Liv has been finishing her assignments. In particular, an interactive narrative for her computer subject. *Liv Walks Home.* It won some award, the university did a big song and dance around it. Six years ago the gridiron helmet that you had to wear to view the thing was really cutting edge. I remember being curious, putting the helmet on, playing the experience. I am sure it is archived somewhere but you wouldn't find one of those helmets anywhere anymore.

It was nothing. Well it was something, obviously, but it wasn't anything that you would expect. It was a representation of a spring day. You walked in the shoes of a young girl. You felt the weight of her textbooks in the backpack on her shoulder. You walked past low-set houses along a footpath and arrived at a metal gate. That is the whole of the story. The thing about it was the wall of jasmine. It was the one moment of pause in the walk. You stopped and looked at the wall of jasmine and it was just bursting into new flower and you took in breath and you smelled it and there was a flood of emotion, the same emotion every time. A sad beauty, a bouquet of ennui. There is still a jasmine bush climbing the wall along Thompson Street. It is on my way home from uni. Of course it is, because that fence is my fence. The Home in the story is my home. She made the narrative for me. She made it so that I would stop and look at the jasmine and smell it and feel something.

I have never been able to walk past that fence in spring without feeling that same bittersweet sense of loss and new beginnings. We were breaking up. I was about to kick her out of my house. Home would no longer be home to Liv. She would never again open that metal gate with the same feeling of arrival.

Liv Walks Home was not even a proper story, but there was a story. Everyone who experienced it felt the echoes of a story even if they didn't know exactly what it was they were feeling.

There is still a glimpse of hope. There is sun on your shoulders. Flowers are emerging from the bud. Things might get better. When you put the helmet on and relaxed into the experience of *Liv Walks Home* you would have the distinct impression that there was no need, perhaps, to hold on to your pervasive feeling of despair. She wasn't the first person to use that technology. Gamers had been using it for months. Now there are people who film their adventures like this. For a price you can climb Mount Everest, paddle around the world in a kayak, trek up a river in Bolivia, go caving into the very depths of the world.

After I have eaten I put the mask back on and check my progress on the bar at the bottom of the screen. I have missed three days of work. I have told them I am ill, and I am. I am sick with this. Or Liv is sick. One of us. I am not even sure how to tell which part of the feeling is me and which is her.

There is only one more chapter. I know how this one ends. I could just skip it altogether. I don't even need to press play, but of course I do.

I am walking home from uni. Sun on my shoulders, dappled under the jacaranda trees. First blooms so purple underfoot. The jasmine wall is in full bloom and some patches of flower have yellowed. Dried blossoms make a pile of dirty snow in the grass below. There is still the smell, still that feeling of nostalgia, but then I reach the gate and my feelings are more complicated now. The weeping sound the hinge makes as it opens is more banshee than siren song. It is only a matter of time—hours—but I am not aware of it as I lift the clasp and settle the gate behind me once more. Our story is almost done. I don't know the details. I don't know about the girl who has been visiting in my absence, but I know. I look down to the cobbled path. I want to remember each irregular stone. I want to stay in this moment but everything is already moving on. He has moved on. I have. I have moved on. I have moved on and my heart is broken for the first time. I have never felt anything like this before.

'I'm sorry.'

I stand before the class. Jane is in her usual place, the rest are still a nameless whole. I look out at each and every one of them and I know how it feels to look down at me from their position. I know how I seem, bigger than I really am, taking up more of their attention than I should. They feign indifference but they all really care so much about what I might think of them. I can change a day with one nod, with a tick in a margin. I could change a life just by taking one of them aside and telling them, keep going. It will all work out for you. Keep going. I could make the next generation of writers, creators, with an easy sentence or two. What have I been doing all this time? I stare out at all the opportunities I have wasted, all the women I have overlooked because they are too fat or too short or too full of fight, all the young men I have seen as competition. I have marked them down for their youth or their false bravado. I stand here and for the first time I feel the weight of them, too much for me to hold and yet I must hold them. I have been entrusted with them.

'I'm sorry,' I say and I suppose they think I am apologising for three lectures wasted. It will be difficult for them to pick up all the content before the exam now. That is all on me.

'We're going to skip ahead,' I say. 'This bit isn't really going to help you with anything. Read pages twenty to forty-five in the dossier in your own time, and we can skip over to page sixty-five…

'I'm sorry,' I say again, and I am looking at Jane. She stares back, frowning, but the frown softens a little and she nods.

'Okay. Character. In the classic hero's journey, the character goes on a quest and is transformed by it. But this is memoir. Do we really think a person learns from their actions? Do they change?'

'No. Sir.' It is a young woman in the second row. She puts up her hand belatedly and I wave it away.

'No?'

'No, sir,' she says.

'Can you think of an example in memoir, in all the books we have read so far, where the character changes?'

Hands are raised. I point to them one by one and they give me their examples and I nod. I force myself to say *good.* I say *good, good, good.* It feels good. It does. I say it some more until all the raised hands are exhausted.

'So if people don't change in real life? Why do they change in a memoir?'

More hands raised. More good students trying to please me. Nothing has changed. They are the same students, I am the same lecturer in the same threadbare jumper, but I am pleased. They have pleased me with their enthusiasm.

I still have her skin on me. I still feel her hurt, her disappointment, her terrible bittersweet scent of ennui.

I wonder if the weeks will scour her body from my skin. I will become myself. I will return to myself unchanged because we don't change, not ever. Or at least, I have not ever before.

*

After the lecture I nod to each and every one of the students as they leave. It might be too late to begin to learn their names but I have picked up a few during the lecture and maybe tomorrow I will remember a few more. How long will it be till I sink back into forgetting? I hope it isn't too soon. I want to try living in her skin for just a while longer.

I walk up to Z Block to the post. I have packaged up the suit, and the little memory stick, a little slice of her memory now shared by me, is nestled in its box on top of it all. I tear a slip of paper from my notebook. I wish I had had the forethought to pick a nice card.

Thank you. I write the words carefully. My handwriting is notoriously hard to read. The students tell me this each semester but in all these years I haven't bothered to change it, to make it any easier to read. I put the note in with the memory stick and close the box. I am about to seal it when I change my mind, open the box. Take out the paper. I pick up the pen and let it hover over the paper. *This is really good work.* I underline good, then cross it out. Above it I write the word *extraordinary.*

It doesn't seem like enough, this one sentence to explain what I have lived through this past week. But there are no words to encapsulate it. You would have to live it. The ordinary wonder of it. The extraordinary wonder.

For what it is worth, I am truly sorry.

Not enough. Not nearly enough.

She will publish it and I will not complain. I won't sue her. I won't comment in interviews. If anybody asks me what

I think I will tell them that it is an extraordinary work.

I press the padded bag to seal it. I hesitate at the automated payment machine. Real mail is so expensive. It is a luxury for birthdays and Christmas. Big department stores use mail for shopping but they always cover the costs and they send the packages by private courier. It is so rare, even now, to send an original artefact and not a 3D printout that you download and print at home.

Maybe I should have written that she had changed me. That I was a better person now. That I would never be that kind of man again. But it probably isn't true. I will probably be returned to myself in time.

I walk home down Thompson Street. It is still winter and the jasmine bush has a million buds, pink pushing to white but none of them quite ready to burst. I pick a bud and crush it between my fingers. It smells of bitter sap and I am a little disappointed, but I stand and stare at the vine anyway and remember what it is like when it is full of flowers. I remember what it is like to be flooded with a sense of hope for the coming months. I almost feel it. Not quite.

I keep walking. I'll make sure I come back in a week, maybe two. It will be easy to remember the feeling more clearly, but will I be remembering? Or experiencing it anew? The flowers will be out by then, the sun will be a little warmer. The wind will be less chill. I will be at a little remove from the last few days. It will be spring, come around once more.

PART 2
RONNIE

WHEN I WAS a child we went to the ocean. It was the happiest time. There was sun. There were my feet in the sand, the heat of it between my splayed toes and then the sudden hard cool at the wave line. I would run back and forth along the tidemarks, laughing when the water tugged the sand out from beneath my toes, running back, frightened but excited by it too, this sense of something more powerful than me waiting to take me out into the abyss.

On those sunlit days my father and my sister raced each other out past the breakers. Their strong backs like two rafts made of muscle, bobbing in parallel, fighting the waves. Winning. They were always in competition with each other, my sister broad shouldered, almost as tall as my father. Bull-headed like my father. Matching him stroke for stroke, and the race to the buoy with very little in it, one hand up and helicoptering down to touch the winning mark a second before the other. The winner would pant and cheer and lie on his or her back and punch a fist towards the impossibly blue sky. The loser would rage and snarl and breaststroke back to shore, snatching up their towel, covering me with a dusting of sand that stung my eyes and gritted between my teeth.

It's that kind of beach. Too bright. Too hot. And I am standing on the shore wondering if these are my memories or someone else's idea of ocean that somehow corresponds with my own. I squint and search the horizon for a buoy, and two strong backs swimming towards it, but the ocean is steady and empty. The breath of water rising and falling as if it were sleeping.

When I was a child I was earth-bound. I was not the same kind of human as my sister and my father. Big seals, both of them, slippery in the surf, uncatchable. Sometimes we would play this game, if you were an animal, and they were dolphins, whales, eels, salmon. I reached for animals like lions or panthers, cats with teeth, but my answers were always lies. If I were an animal I would be a pipi. My toes dig for them now in the cold wet sand, as a wave comes and snatches the sand away. I am now, as I was then, a furtive, hard-shelled crustacean dumbly waiting for a wave to take the sand from under my feet. Wanting more than anything to dig down into the cold dark, out of sight, out of mind.

To begin this experiment I will need to swim. This is what she told me, detailing the journey, carefully letting me know what to expect. Her name is Liv. They took me to her in a room with a table. A floral tablecloth, a pot of tea, sugar cubes, milk in a jug. I almost sobbed to see it laid out like that, these ordinary trappings of an ordinary life. An ordinary middle-aged woman with dark hair pulled severely back into a ponytail. Her hair was a little long for someone her age; some grey in it. No make-up. She narrowed her eyes when she saw my face for the first time. It was swollen and bruised on the right-hand side. That is pretty common. People like me get hit in prison. People like me deserve to get hit, and prison gives us what we deserve.

Liv was dressed in army boots and a shapeless linen dress. When she lifted her arms there was hair there. I noticed it with a start as if the sight of armpit hair had sent a little pulse of electricity through me. It was vaguely sexual, that unexpected pubic thatch. And then the slippery slope of association tumbling me down to the inevitable. I looked at her armpits and I thought of her crotch and the patch under her arm might as well have been the little triangle between her legs and then again she might shave it and thinking of the hairless place...

I shellfish down into myself, now as I did then when I met her, curling up into the calcium carbonate whorls of me. She is monitoring my thoughts. I try to think of nothing. To unremember the lift of her arm. But when you try to not think of something you fail. The only way out is to replace this thought with another.

This is the only reason I am able to wade out, up to my waist in water. I do it to distract myself. A slap of cold shrivelling my genitals up into a tiny useless packet inside my swimming trunks.

Good.

It is Liv's voice in my head and I can't be sure if I put it there or if she is speaking to me. She will be in my head. She will be with me, that's what she said and I agreed to it. I said yes. Anything to escape that place. To suspend my sentence.

Good work, Ronnie. Now you will have to duck your head under. Remember, it's okay. You will be able to breathe.

Sentences. Hers. I nod. Will she be able to see me nodding?

I've been briefed. She talked me through the process and then we lived it. The first part of it anyway. In the simulation Liv drove me in a car. I'm not sure why there were details like the empty chip packet on the floor, the rattle of a water bottle marking the sharp turns along the windy road, the broken window that only wound up halfway, letting the air conditioning out and the scent of salt and sand in.

There was no car.

She drove me in a car but there was no car. I spent the whole drive trying to get my head around it. Nothing was real and yet she was real, but not real in the way you would expect. She was driving me to the ocean just like my dad used to drive us, only there was no car and no ocean and she was with me but not in any way that I could really understand. It was something to do with my brain. When I counted down from ten I was falling asleep like you would for any operation, only waking in a car didn't mean I was awake in the real world.

There was no car. And yet I stepped out of the car and she leaned out of the drivers window and she touched my arm and I started to cry.

This is okay. You are okay. I'll be watching. I'll be with you. When you make contact I will be monitoring the contact. Don't worry. It will feel strange, but I'll be here.

Put your head under the water now. She says this and she isn't really talking. Or there isn't really any water. I try to imagine myself in some high-tech room with monitors and machines that beep and a screen with my brainwaves on it. Liv, maybe sitting in front of the console, talking into a headset, or maybe sitting beside my hospital bed, talking to me, or typing the words. She briefed me but I didn't ask all the questions, or the right questions. Yes, I said, I understand. But I didn't really understand.

A wave comes in and rushes against my chest and I feel my heart racing. I feel the panic coming. I am at the beach and my sister and my father are out there, racing each other. I have wandered into the water but I won't put my head under. I am not genetically wired for water as they are. I am someone else's son, no matter what they call me or what I call them. They're dolphining out past the breakers and I take a deep and panicked breath. I feel my shell slamming shut. I feel the grit of sand in my mouth. I duck down under the water in my awkward clam-like way.

She said I would be able to breathe.

There is no water.

I am in a room hooked up to monitors.

I am not here at all.

Nothing here is real, and yet if that's so, what if nothing in my other, real, world is real either? Do I need to worry about what is really happening? Does anything happen at all?

I unhinge my shell and there is water. I open my mouth and there is water.

I struggle. I am drowning.

My sister held me down and I knew she was laughing but I couldn't hear it because she was bobbing at the surface and I was down on the grate of sandy bottom trying not to breathe.

Breathe, Liv tells me. Breathe normally. It will be okay.

Liv and my sister in the bright sunshine, holding my head under the water till I know I will die from lack of breath. My sister reaching inside my swim shorts. My sister grabbing hold of me and laughing, laughing.

And I breathe.

Everything hurts with water. My head throbs. My lungs ache. I hear the beep, beep, beep of the waves thrashing against me. Waves don't beep.

I am in pain.

Waves hush.

Shhh, she says. It's all right. Shhh, shhh, shhh.

And I hear the waves hushing like a heartbeat, steady, rhythmic, calm now.

I am under the waves. When I look up they are a churn of light and air above me. If I stand, my head will be back in the air. I don't want to have to learn to breathe again and so I crawl as the sand dips down, sloping towards deeper water. My hands and knees chafe against the ground. I feel vaguely weightless. I float a little, breathe out. Settle back down onto the ocean floor. One knee after the other, shuffling down, down to the deeper water. At a certain point I can stand up, so that's what I do. Walking is less effort. I bounce from one step to the next. I never walked underwater when I was a child. I never got to sit on the bottom of the pool.

My sister would hold her knees to her flat chest, her powerful brown arms tasting of salt because even the hotel pool was a nod to the ocean. I remember tasting the salt on her arms. My sister would open her eyes and stare up at me with her hair like a jellyfish undulating out from her face. I would be at the edge of the pool, not even my feet in the water. If I let my feet down she would lunge up and grab them and pull me down to where I might drown. I sat in the sun and watched her, wanting nothing more than to reach in and feel the waving of her hair.

I stand in the water and stare around. I am looking for jellyfish. I am looking for the strands of her hair.

Liv told me I would not see the jellyfish, and of course she's right, but I feel my body sitting strange in the water. I feel my skin respond to the tug of the tide. I'm tangled in her hair or in the memory of her hair or in the memory of being a jellyfish. I'm not sure which.

Keep walking. Those were my instructions. Keep walking and the puzzle will present itself to me. To us, because there are two of us solving the conundrum. Me and this strange otherworldly creature. Apparently it will need both of us to solve it.

I walk underwater and I'm sure I must already be paired

with the jellyfish. I thought maybe I would see it, like a halo around me. I would feel a coating of gelatinous stuff cushioning my limbs. But no. It's just this weightlessness. This bouncing forward through water.

Liv told me they'd almost made a jellyfish from scratch in the lab. Rat cells, she said. The heart cells of a rat, specifically. Cellulose...or celluloid? Something. And then an electric current to animate the thing like Frankenstein's monster. The brain is a simple collection of cells so it should have been easy enough to make this robot monster behave just like its aquatic counterparts. But the creature that resulted moved like a jellyfish for maybe a few hours, pumping its jelly body up and down in a tank, until it stopped, sank to the top and floated there, inert, refusing to eat, refusing to reproduce, dead to the world. The jellyfish should have lived but it didn't. I don't know why she told me this.

'There was something missing,' she told me. 'I was monitoring its robot brain. It felt like something was missing. From the inside of that brain it felt like...' She shook her head. 'It felt...Well, we don't know why it didn't work. This will be the first time a human is paired with a non-human. You'll be making history.'

I'm thinking about this when it happens. I'm thinking about how I could go from drowning on the ocean floor with my sister's hair jellyfishing around me to being here, making history. I'm wondering why someone like me is chosen to make history.

And then it happens. A shift. A lurch, and my stomach

lurches with it. Even in this virtual space I think I'm going to vomit. I am...propelled. Suddenly. I'm not sure what's happening but the world shifts. I've entered a video game and I am pixelated. Or perhaps something has taken me apart cell by cell and distributed the pieces of my body around the universe.

I close my eyes, but that's worse. I am seasick.

'Stop,' I say. 'Stop this.'

It's okay, she says. This is the pairing.

It's clear that what I felt when I first walked into the virtual ocean is not what's happening now. I can sense something else inside my body. It's as if an earwig crawled inside my head to chatter in my brain. Or, no, not like that because this feeling isn't located just in my head. I'm not sure I have an actual head anymore, or if I do I'm not inside it anymore. I'm located elsewhere. I am located in a thousand elsewheres.

What does it feel like? she asks me. Can you put it into words?

'Like...like I've been exploded.'

I don't understand.

'Fragments. See? There are fragments of me everywhere.'

I become used to the feeling incrementally. I am embodied once more. And here it is, a maze, like a hedge maze only made of sand. This is the puzzle I am supposed to solve. Not alone. I am not alone. When I hold out my hand I feel it clasped by another hand. I can't see anyone there but it feels like someone is holding me. Then...there's an echo of that feeling. It feels as if I have a hundred hands and each of them is being taken, by more and more hands. I have never felt less alone as I take my first step towards the walls of sand and slip between them. It's hard for the light to penetrate here, between the sand walls. It's dark. I move along with my hands outstretched and I can feel the grit against my fingers. I'm leading the way but I feel the slow drag of other people behind me. My sister maybe, my father, their bodies anchored to me. It's my job to make sure they both drag along behind.

I feel a corner with my fingertips and I pull us forward towards it. The pleasure of rounding the corner is like an electric shock. I feel my skin buzz and prickle.

Now the sand walls widen out. It gets darker. I see them disappearing into the void. I feel a momentary panic.

I can't see. I can't hear, I can't feel. I am lost. There is no body for me to be inside. I open what might be my mouth but instead of voice there's an electric static. Not a sound, but a feeling. And with this electric jolt I have a sense of my body in the ocean and I know I have to turn to the right to find the plankton.

Finding the plankton is all-important. I didn't know that was what I was searching for, but now it seems impossible that I didn't want it before. The hunger rages through my body, through all of the bodies. All of the bodies. There's not just me. I am many.

'I am multiplied.' I didn't mean to speak and the sound of my voice surprises me.

What? Liv is still with me.

I struggle to find the words. 'I am not one. I am many.'

I don't understand.

'I am all of us. I am...plural.'

Yes. Your mind is hooked up with the jellyfish. You are networked. There are two of you in there.

'No. Not two. I don't know...Maybe...There is one other I suppose but it's so large...and it stretches over and across the whole ocean. I can feel the ocean. All of it. I am all the jellyfishes...Networked, that's the word for it. I'm networked, like the internet, but I'm in all the computers everywhere. Not like I'm paired with one creature. Not exactly. I am all of us; we are...me. I'm one and all at the same time. It doesn't make any sense, does it?'

I wait for her reply but she's silent. There is only the non-sound of all of me, cell by pulsing cell. Feeling one with the others and feeling one and only at the same time.

So many of me, and yet only one of me and I'm hungry. I know my place in the water, not because I can see or hear or feel, I know where I am because of my relationship to the other parts of me. I find my way through the maze, sending out electrical impulses, knowing because we are many that I'm heading in the right direction. I navigate the twists and turns so easily and then when I come to the feeding room I reach for the plankton and I'm feeding and somehow the rest of me feels fed by the very act of my eating. I am nourishing the many and the one.

Gosh that was quick, says Liv.

I hear her voice and she is so far away from me. Separate

from me. My father is separate from me. My sister, separate.

So you feel like there is more than one consciousness in your head?

'I have more than one head. I am all of them, all at once.'

She's quiet. Distant. She is separate from me.

We're going to bring you back now. Do you remember how we said it would be?

I remember.

My body is empty of plankton. The maze has disappeared. It never existed in the first place. I turn and walk along the surface of the ocean. I will return to myself.

Soon.

It has only been a matter of minutes, or maybe hours. It's hard to tell. All I know is that when I walked into the ocean I was alone, when I walk out I'm one of many. It's a kind of connection I have never dreamed of making. I'm more than the sum of myself. I walk towards the light, which is streaming in through a soupy mess of kelp. The light touches my skin and I shiver. We're all shivering. We are walking towards the light and the electric charge of sunlight excites us.

There are waves up there in the near distance, breaking on gravelly sand. I remember being held underwater. My sister's head blocking the sun. Trying to breathe. Trying to breathe underwater. I walk towards it all and the ocean churns above me. Too close. I duck, but am sucked up into a rolling wave. I'm turned upside down, I feel the scrape along my back, my arms. And my sister's face, her strong swimmer's arms.

And it hurts. I am rolled, I can't breathe. I want them to stop me from breathing. I want to stay in the ocean but there is no ocean. There never was any ocean. And I'm awake and my sister is leaning over my bed, her hair hanging down around her face, the light turning it into a halo.

'Are you okay?' she says, but it isn't my sister's voice. It's Liv. Liv's voice.

I'm alone. More alone now because I know what it is to not be alone. I'm crying. I feel the sobbing rack my body. I feel ill with it. I might vomit.

'What's wrong?' She touches my forehead. Her fingers connect me to the world.

I want my sister.

I don't want my sister.

'Tell me what's wrong.'

'I didn't know how alone we are until now. I didn't know,' I say.

She takes her fingers off my forehead and there is just me, lying on a hospital bed. I miss my sister more than I ever have but if she were here in the room now I might reach up to her and wrench her head off her broad brown shoulders.

I pace. The cell seems smaller after my outing to the beach. I am calling it an outing and it feels like I've gone on some kind of journey, even if it was in my head. Why can't they just make a machine and plug in all the long-term prisoners? We could feel like we were out for the day and no one would need to keep an eye on us. We would just be hooked up to the machine. What if they have already made this machine? What if we are hooked up already? What if everyone in the world is hooked up to it and prison is all in our heads, what if we're just lying on a hospital bed just like everyone else in the world? What if it's all an illusion, these bars, this small containment, this endless day repeated every time I wake. Isn't that the plot of a film I once saw? What if we are all in some virtual film and the film within our film is to tease us?

Of course, there are variations. Today I have therapy to look forward to. They ask me about sex. I don't feel like sex. I never feel like having sex anymore. They give me monthly injections and there's no sex left in me after that. But I remember wanting it. In an hour, when they take me to my appointment, we'll talk about that.

I sit at my desk and there are books here. At one time I was pretending I was studying, that I was doing a law degree by correspondence. Every second person here long term is doing their law degree by correspondence. I still have some law texts but now there are more history books, books about wars, books about presidents and climbers and, yes, swimmers. I flick through a book about an Olympic swimmer and there are photos of his sister in a swimming costume. I remember my sister in a swimming costume. Only in our story she would be the athlete standing in the next photo with a medal looped around her neck. I would be the brother in his swim trunks, laughing and slapping her on the back.

*

Somehow an hour goes by. This has changed since my participation in the experiment. Time. Something odd has happened to it. It has taken on physical form. Time rubs up against me like an invisible film, like Glad Wrap but the whole roll of it goes on and on forever. There is so much plastic wrap stretching out behind me, and in front of me, an age of it. I feel like I am trapped under an invisible film, staring out, perfectly preserved. I am not sure why time feels so different but something has shifted in the way I wait for things.

The hour passes. They come for me. Cuff me. I am used to all of this, the walk from the cell to the psych room, with its vague smell of piss and disinfectant. Sometimes one of the psychs sees me more than once but mostly there's someone new in the chair every time I'm led inside.

This time it's Liv.

This genuinely surprises me. I stand in the doorway with my mouth gaping.

She smiles. She's in my house—I live here and she doesn't—but she asks me to sit down. She flattens her hands out on the surface of the table. Heavy, wood, bolted to the floor if you peer underneath it but from above it's just a table, the kind you might gather your family around to share dinner. A thanksgiving table. She bunches her fingers into a fist and knocks on it, frowns and nods. She crosses her arms on the table and leans her head against them and looks sideways at the wall, which is scuffed and marked, and I see her looking at an actual shoe print that has not been scrubbed away or painted over.

She stares hard at the footprint and stretches her right hand out along the table as if she is mentally measuring the size of it against her fingers.

'You know,' Liv says, 'in our lifetimes there will be nothing large left in the ocean except cephalopods and jellyfish.'

I nod. I remember my sister and my father, their strong backs, racing. I used to worry about sharks. Maybe one day I would be watching and a shark would take them. I would see one of them rise up, hands flailing, then disappear, tugged under the swell. The other would look back at me standing safely on the beach, startled. Their arms would reach out, pulling their body through the water. They would begin to swim. Then they, too, would be gone.

She's been speaking but I've been lost to thoughts of an ocean full of sharks. 'Cockroaches,' she has said. 'Weeds.'

'...like coral,' she's saying now, 'attached to the ocean floor. Or they can attach to debris, power plants, rigs, anything made by humans or naturally forming. They attach themselves there, and then, when the conditions are right, they send out the jellyfish parts of themselves. Do you understand?'

I shake my head.

'Maybe I'm not explaining it properly. I don't really know the science of it that well, but basically each different type of jellyfish is just one big colony. Each individual swimming medusa that we recognise as a jellyfish is one part of a bigger creature. These creatures are so alien to anything we understand that we have made the wrong assumptions about them for decades. Each colony is over six million years old.' She makes a small gesture. 'This is a relatively new understanding of them.'

'So you didn't hook me up to a jellyfish?' When she explained the experiment to me the first time I'd imagined them sticking probes into the creature in a big tank.

'We did. But your idea of jellyfish might be a bit different to the reality. Have you heard of quantum entanglement?'

I shake my head.

'Spooky action?'

Liv can tell she's losing me. She shrugs. 'It's not important. It's just that we've figured some things out using quantum entanglement and when you were hooked up to the jellyfish you were hooked up to a much larger thing. A six-million-year-old collection of interlinked parts. Maybe older. Probably older.'

She's quite pretty. I imagine that a dozen years or so ago she would have been quite a looker, as they used to say. She still has all these girlish gestures, drumming her fingers on the table, shifting her body up in the chair and then slumping down again. She seems like a restless child, but she's firmly middle-aged and her tunic stretches tight at the waist. She has thickened, as women do later in life. This is how I've always imagined my mother would be if she were still alive: thick-set but pretty, practical, caring, filled with laughter. I wonder what my sister looks like now. I wonder if she has begun to gentle into plump matronhood. She was always just a block of solid muscle with a will that spurred her body on like a rechargeable battery.

'Are you following any of this?'

I shake my head.

'Do you want to follow any of this?'

'Something feels strange since the thing.'

She sits up straight for once and stares directly at me, waiting. Listening. It's a bit unnerving. I feel like the centre of her universe in this moment.

She says nothing and so I hesitantly continue.

'It feels like I'm in plastic wrap. Like, preserved. Do you know what I mean?'

She nods, all eyes, all ears.

'I feel like every minute is longer than it used to be but also shorter. I feel like it doesn't matter how long a day takes anymore.'

She nods again.

'And also…'

When she's waited for what must be several minutes she puts out her hand and caresses the table as if it might be my arm, calming me by osmosis through the warm wood.

'You should talk about this. You are unique. You're the first person who's tried this. We've done it with monkeys and dolphins, and hooked cats up to dogs, but a jellyfish colony? This is something new. These are our future, the jellyfish. When everything else is dead there will still be a hundred billion of them drifting about in the water.'

'Lonely,' I say. 'I feel lonely. But not like, first week in a new city, gotta write home kind of lonely. Something…else.'

She sits back suddenly. She turns her attention to the

shoe print on the wall. She purses her lips.

'We want to do it one more time, hook you up, you know. We want to try something. We think it might be a cure.'

'What for?'

She nods to my lap and I feel the colour rising in my cheeks. Of course she knows my history. She would have read about my crimes. The whole sordid tragedy. When she nods towards my groin we both know what she's talking about.

The bruises on my cheeks, my ribs, they've all healed but there will be more bruises, more broken ribs when the rapes start again. They're like clockwork. Not every day, not even every week, but eventually they come round again and I just close my eyes and endure because that's what I deserve. What they all hear about me is true. What they all dish out is what I have coming to me.

'When?'

'Next week?'

'Will you take me out of here to wait? Will you put me someplace safe?'

She looks around the room. She raps her knuckles on the surface of the table.

'I have the authority to make that happen.'

'Thank you,' I tell her. I begin to stand. She holds up her hands to stop me, eases them up and down as if she were patting me on my shoulder. I settle back into the chair.

'We need to do a psych assessment first. We need to make sure you're up to it. I need to bring a psychologist in. Is that okay with you?'

I nod.

'I want to stay. I don't have to. I can leave, but I really want to stay and make sure this is not going to hurt you in any way.'

'All right,' I say. 'I want you to stay.'

She smiles. She presses the buzzer that is usually there to protect them from us. She is alerting the guard. When the door opens she nods and it closes again.

'I hope we can help you,' she says. 'It would be the least we could do. You volunteered for something that might have gone fairly badly. It didn't. It worked out fine. I hope we can fix some things for you in return.'

I can feel my heart beating too fast. I don't want to hope. Hope has always led to the terrible weight of disappointment. I try not to feel anything as we wait for her psychologist. I concentrate on the footprint on the wall. Someone else's pain, someone else's story. Stories never have a happy ending, that's one thing I've learnt. I wonder if that's what she's thinking when she looks at it. Stories never turn out well and the boot print is just one more indication of a single tragedy in among the many. She looks back at me and smiles, and I can tell that isn't what she was thinking at all.

It was one summer or it was all summers. It seemed to stretch on and on. You could bite into me and it would be like biting into a cheap strawberry-filled chocolate: the rest of my life just a thin wall. My adult life dissolves so quickly, and then there's nothing but the sweetness of summer, obliterating all the nuances of life with its one note. Watching my family swim away from me, fighting waves, fighting each other: completely oblivious of my existence. My sister's attention. Her hair tumbling down to fan about my face in the water. The suffocation. Holding my breath till I am dizzy. Her rough hands around my neck. Those hands grabbing at my penis in the water. It's all so cloyingly sweet that it makes me gag when I think about it. Maybe I was five years old or six or seven and maybe that summer dragged on and on until I shrugged childhood off and dragged myself to high school, university, my first job. I can't be sure because it is all the one flavour and it is everything that is inside me. I'm empty of all other experiences.

I avoid the beach now. At least that's one less thing I have to miss since I was arrested. Even before the arrest I tried hard to avoid the beach where the little girls run to the edge of the surf with their perfect skin and their wide, frightened eyes. Where if they leap in, laughing and stroking the waves as hard as my sister, I know they are not mine. If they hesitate, if they stand with the water tugging the sand out from under their toes; if they hop from foot to foot and goosebumps fan up and over their shoulders, then I know they are of me. My heart feels like a fist in my chest. The clench of all my organs, the clench in my crotch.

I tell her this because she is here to help me. I tell the stranger and there is Liv, impassive, sitting close behind. I tell them about how I crouch down on one knee and whisper them into the water. *See? It's okay. You just have to trust, and hold my hand and it doesn't feel so bad.* There are waves but I put my back to them and they break over me and the little frightened girl is safe in my shadow.

Inside me there is only the bright light of summer and my sister laughing at me and the sense that I am drowning. Each of the girls is exactly my age, some indeterminate summer age, still struggling to find her feet when the water is already above her head. Each one of the girls swims with me here, her little churning body bumping up against mine. When they emerge from the water, panting, their small arms aching from the desperate arcs they have made in unfamiliar water, when they run run run up the beach away from the bad man, they have already learnt to swim. *Sometimes,* my sister tells me as she climbs out onto the sand after me, *you need to be dropped in the deep water before you can learn to save yourself.*

All the girls I have saved, hurt, frightened, saved, hurt, saved. All the girls who I have taught to swim.

Liv looks down at me and she counts back from ten. She is holding my hand. She knows all about me and yet she can meet my eyes with her own and she can hold my gaze. I could love a woman like this. I have never really entertained the idea of love. I wasn't built for it.

As she says the word *seven* I'm watching her lips. Maybe her mouth could save me from this bone-cold engulfing loneliness. She says *six*. She is counting my birthdays. She is locating me in history. *Five.* And there's nothing earlier. We have reached the end of the middle and it's hot by the beach where we are lying side by side.

She is wearing a one-piece swimsuit. My sister always wore bikinis. She loved the sun on her tight athlete's stomach. She loved the way her skin remembered the shape of her swimwear even when she was naked. She could remain in her togs all winter just by taking her clothes off and admiring the fading tan line in the mirror. I know. I saw her do it. It was her way of taking us back to the surf and the sand.

Liv is so far from being my sister that when I roll over I put out my hand. She takes it. She knows about me but she takes my hand. I could weep or I could hug her, but I do neither of these things. I lie on my side holding her hand and I listen.

'How do you feel?'

She has a thick waist. Cellulite disfiguring her thighs. Her ankles are thick. Her toes are short and the toenails have the traces of nail polish on them, blue, almost rubbed away. Her upper arms are beginning to sag. She clearly doesn't work out. She's so unlike my sister that she might as well be an alien species.

'I feel lonely,' I tell her. My world has been reduced to this one fact. I am alone. I will always be alone.

'Not for much longer,' she says. 'When you walk into the water you'll be connected again. Are you ready to experience that?'

I nod.

She lets go of my hand.

'Okay. Go on.'

I stand. Sand is clinging to my back and I dust it away. The breeze takes it in her direction and she coughs and spits and slaps at her face to remove the grit from her eyes. I don't know why this detail is necessary. I don't know why, when I look now, I can see that she hasn't shaved her bikini line. My attention is taken by a pair of pubic hairs that I can see wiring their way out from the elastic of her swimming costume. A disconcerting detail. I'm staring at her crotch; she twists her body, pulling her knees together and the hairs disappear between her thighs.

'Go on.'

I walk towards the ocean. My feet in the cold of it. The water is a wall, an impasse. I can't move forward. I stand and stare out to the horizon. My sister will be there somewhere, my father. Two heads bobbing, two sets of arms cartwheeling easily, joyfully through the surf.

'Here. Come with me.'

She takes my hand and she is running with me. The water slaps at my crotch. I jump, trying to stay above it. I struggle to swim but she is walking through the waves, she is pulling me down and under.

Come with me.

Her head completely submerged. Me gasping, bobbing up above the water. Her hand like the rope on an anchor. I take a deep breath. I let her lead me down.

Let go. You can breathe. Remember? You did it before. You can breathe.

I stare down at her. Shorter and thicker than my sister, her body rounded in places where she was tight and firm. She's pale, too, as if she's never spent a summer in the sun.

Take a breath.

And I do. And I can breathe. I'm not drowning.

She lets go of my hand and she waves as if I am going on a journey and she walks backwards, back through the waves. She walks away. My sister swims away.

I can breathe. I'm alive still, but I could die of this hollow inside me. It's the loneliness that will kill me. I gulp in water like someone with a death wish. Is that what this is?

Then they spawn.

That is what it's like, thousands of them multiplying in my chest. All of them making up one of them, making up me. I'm a person, plural. I am more of myself. It buoys me. I'm floating up to the surface of the water. Bobbing just under the waterline. Somewhere my sister might be swimming towards me. My father will be in her wake or maybe he'll reach me first, maybe that will change the course of things.

Hold tight. Know you are safe. I'm watching over you.

It is Liv's voice. Liv, swimming towards me, touching the buoy of me. Touching home. I feel her hand on my soft carapace. I feel the disturbance of her presence, and I drift away from her. But she's following.

Then a shadow.

Then teeth.

Then pain.

When a *Turritopsis dohrnii* is attacked it has the unique ability to regress. Her voice, soothing. She is reciting from a textbook or telling me what she has read.

Teeth.

My heart beating so fast it might explode, a soft pulsing medusa out of my chest.

It will change at a genetic level. It will transform back to its juvenile polyp state. Do you understand?

And all of me arse up and about. My sister swimming away from me. Liv, holding me, whispering to me and my sister, my father, disappearing towards the dorsal fin of a…

Shark.

Shark or fish or boat with its motor knifing too close to me, into the flesh of me. Teeth.

No other creature does this, says Liv. The *Turritopsis dohrnii* is unique. Because of this we don't know how old each individual medusa is—perhaps they never die. This is why we call it the immortal jellyfish.

And my sister's fingertips breaking the surface of the water. I can see them. She is falling up, into the sky, out of my reach. I reach. I breathe through the pain of it. Breathing water, surviving despite the taste of salt and weed in my throat. I am five and I am learning to swim for the first time. I am four. I am standing at the edge of the ocean. I am stamping my feet in the foam. I am three. I am crying. I have a blue string wrapped around my ankle and the skin turning red where the jellyfish stings. I am two. I'm happy. I'm free of all of it and there is my mother. I had forgotten my mother. She's wearing a one-piece swimming costume. She's thick waisted, thick ankled. She is smiling. She's touching my forehead, touching the jellyfish body of me. Hushing me. And I am safe.

You are safe. I am still here with you. You're safe.

I am safe.

When the immortal jellyfish is attacked it moves backwards in time, at least on a cellular level. Then, when it's safe, it is free to grow into an adult again.

I am free. I am growing.

I am five. I am seven. I am twelve, thirteen, twenty. There is the relief of adulthood. I am growing out of the body I used to inhabit. I'm not sure who I'll be when the tide turns, but I know I'm safe.

You are safe. I have you. It's okay.

I am many. I am immortal. I am regrown. I am okay.

I hear her counting. From two she counts me up. Ten, she says and, reluctantly, I open my eyes. She has her hand on my forehead. She's meeting my gaze. I am a monster and she is meeting my gaze firmly, solidly with her own.

'How do you feel?'

And I am still pulsing. I'm moving like a jellyfish moves. No, I'm lying still and only my jellyfish chest is moving, pulsing up and down in an effort to escape. No. It is just the heaving of my lungs as I weep.

'It's okay,' she says. 'You're safe with me. How do you feel?'

'Alone. I am so alone.'

'I'm here,' she says, which is true but it is only her and

she is separate from me. I was one and many and now I'm just me. It's tragic. It is unbearable.

'Are you okay?'

I try to stop my chest from jellyfishing. I try to breathe without drowning. I nod.

'We are going to take you back to your room.'

'Prison?'

'No. Your room, here in the research facility.'

I nod. Relieved.

'When you've recovered we're going to run some tests. Is that okay?'

I nod.

She stands and I reach out to catch her hand. I don't want her to go. I really don't want her to go.

When she is holding my hand I am still alone.

When she lets go I am alone.

This loneliness is all I know. I look out to the horizon and I'm sure my sister is still there somewhere, only there was an attack, a shark or some other fish, and maybe she was taken. Maybe she was all I had and she was taken. When you bite into me I am a hollow, the disappointment of a chocolate rabbit at Easter. Stale and tasteless on the outside; and inside, nothing but a space in the shape of another, absent rabbit.

I have sat for their tests before. When I take my place in the seat and look away while they put the rubber tubing on my cock I'm filled with a familiar shame. I hate myself. Moving right along. Nothing to see here.

They start with rabbits humping. A horse with an erection that reaches down to his hooves. Then a woman, naked, posing like a *Playboy* model. I am unmoved. No. Maybe a little bit moved. I could be persuaded to be moved. I'm sure they're recording these minuscule changes. A tiny swelling, a movement of the blood. But maybe it's my fear, not my arousal, nudging the rubber tube outward. They show me a picture of a man, similar pose; boxer shorts, muscles. I really don't care for this kind of thing. I concentrate on the emptiness, the deep bone-melting ache in the centre of me. I can't shake it. I can't sleep for it.

They show me a picture of an older woman. Clothed, but with a low-cut top. Her hair is pulled back and it's turning grey. She reminds me of Liv. I wonder where Liv is now. I wish she was the one putting the pictures up on the screen. I wish she was the one measuring the rising and falling of my penis. Rising. I look at the photo which isn't Liv but might be her sister and my penis is rising. This is a surprise. I am aroused by her. I sit with the pleasant feeling. Wide eyed.

They take their readings and move on. An older man. A soft deflation. I have never been attracted to men. I think of my father and I can't even see his face anymore, just the pistoning of muscles. I see his back and his ropey neck. My erection subsides.

Boy child. And there is a tiny rush of fear that might or might not affect the readings on their instruments. I am not aroused by the boy child but I am disturbed by the sight of him, shirtless, tiny shorts, tiny Converse shoes.

Girl child. The warning bells are beating a rhythmic throb in my head. This is my weakness. This is where I will out myself...

I glance down at the limp hang of my penis. I don't understand what has happened. This is what betrays me every time I take this test.

Girl child. Nothing.

Adolescent girl. Nothing.

Adolescent boy. Nothing.

Adult woman. Nothing.

Adult man. Nothing.

Liv, or a Liv-ish woman. A little rise. An interest, you might say.

Older man. Nothing.

Dog. No.

Cat. No.

Horse. No.

Fish. And I feel a flicker of something.

Octopus. Is it fear?

Jellyfish. And I come.

One minute I am watching the delicate undulations of her mantle, the play of light as she broadcasts her readiness in the currents of the water and then I am ejaculating. I didn't even have time to register my arousal. I sit in it. This is the heat of my shame rising across my chest and up my neck.

I am ridiculous.

The test is over. The assistant takes the rubber sheath off cautiously. What a job to have to do.

They say nothing, and that's almost worse. They allow me to dress myself and they walk me back to my room. Soon it will be replaced by the cell I've been living in for three years. I open the door myself. The simple pleasures. They lock it behind me.

I'm lonely.

I don't know how long I lie on my bed feeling lonely.

When Liv knocks and opens the door I swing my legs off the bed and pull the pillow closer. She isn't beautiful; she isn't young. And yet she's a tiny crack in my loneliness. She comes straight over and sits beside me. It's nice to feel the shift of the bed as it adjusts to her weight. I could make love with her. I know I could, and not the abortive attempts of my university days. I could lie down with her and my body could fit around hers. Her body could fit around mine. We wouldn't be as one but we would be as close as two people can come. She's been inside my head. She's been inside me. If I reached out and touched her thigh now it wouldn't be as intimate as what we have shared.

'So, did you cure me?'

She doesn't look at me. She looks at her shoes: heavy black boots. There are scuff marks on the toe of the right one. I stare at that place. I've seen that before but I am not sure where or what caused it. Kicking something? Does she play some kind of sport in those shoes?

She shrugs. 'You don't seem to display the same kind of attraction to prepubescents.'

'No.' And the truth of the experiment is hanging like a grey cloud between us. 'I want to go back.'

She nods.

'I'm not sure what data you're getting or whatever. I'm not sure how well your experiment is going, but I'd like to go back.'

She nods once more. 'We weren't intending on hooking you up again. We have some more testing to do but I think we'll find you will not reoffend. I don't think you'll be going back to prison, if that's what you are afraid of.'

Her knee is so close to mine I can feel the warmth of it. I put my hand down between our legs and the back of it touches her.

She looks up, frowns, but there's a sweetness in her eyes that makes it more a frown of sympathy than of anger.

We will never make love.

'So you won't send me back?'

'To prison?'

'To the ocean.'

She shifts her hips and her leg falls away from my hand and my hand feels cold. I fold it into my lap, wrap my fingers around it.

'I'm sure we can. I'll check. I imagine it will be useful for us. But what if it upsets the balance? We took you back. We bypassed whatever it was that went wrong. I don't think you will be reoffending ever again. I really think we might have fixed that now.'

The cold travels up my arm. It fills me. I shiver.

'If you can arrange for it, I would like to be hooked up one more time.'

She looks into my eyes for the first time. She holds my gaze. I wonder what she sees there. I wonder if she sees the empty space inside me where another person is missing. I wonder if she realises that the other person is me. I'm not here anymore. I have disappeared.

'Okay,' she says, 'I'll find out.'

She reaches over and she hugs me. I can feel the catch in my throat as her hands close around my shoulders. It's a quick hug, and it takes me by surprise. I don't have time to hug her back. I put my arm up and tap her back awkwardly, and she's gone. There is a lingering smell of petrol. Then I remember. My sister rode a motorcycle and there was always that worn place on the toe of her boot where she changed gears.

Liv rides a motorcycle.

It's a surprise to me. I don't know anything about her. She's a person separate from me and what we have shared has everything to do with my head and nothing to do with her at all. She stands and smiles and I smile back and it's just the surface of ourselves, a thin communication.

When she leaves I am still alone. Always alone. I lie on my bed and try to understand the passing of time. It isn't urgent. I have the rest of my life to figure it all out, or I have forever. Each minute that passes is just a tiny piece of now. I wonder how so much absence can fit into such an insignificant parcel of time.

*

Liv is swimming. Liv is one stroke ahead of me and I can see her back tensing against a wave, her feet kicking. She looks younger in the water. More lithe. But she doesn't swim like my sister used to swim. Water is not her element. She stops and treads water and I can see the top of her swimming costume on her shoulder is twisted. I almost reach out and straighten it but I stop myself just in time.

'You're sure?' She pushes wet hair back behind her ear, panting. A swell comes and she rises up and drops down again and then I'm caught in it and it pushes me away from her so I have to stroke a couple of times to reach her.

'One more time. Just this one time.'

It's difficult for me to stay up here at the surface with her. How easy would it be to duck-dive, to push down through the water, to find the sandy bottom of the ocean.

I turn and there is the beach such a long way away. I squint to look at the bright stretch of sand. It is like looking at the sun. There is a child on the beach, an adult squatting close. The child runs into a wave and then runs back into the waiting arms of a parent. I try to remember my sister, but all that seems like another lifetime.

I take a breath and duck my head down under the water then bob up again.

'Thanks,' I say, spitting sea water.

'What for?'

'For setting me free.'

She looks back towards the beach and her forehead knits up as the child squeals. I can hear it, even here beyond the breakers. 'We'll need time to see if that's true. More tests. But you'll live in the facility while they do them.'

'They?'

'They'll be moving me. Into robotics,' she says, 'for my sins.' And then she laughs.

'What is it you do again?'

'Stories,' she says. 'I tell stories. Other people's stories.'

'My story. Does it have a happy ending?'

The swell lifts her and carries her away from me. She strokes back against the wave but it is strong and she's already caught in it.

All endings are arbitrary. Her voice sounds loud in my head. Even if a character dies, that's just the ending we choose. There is more to the story, the body goes on, changes, becomes other, but we've grown tired of the story, or we've taken what we need from it and are ready to move on. I always remember something I read when I was younger. A poet wrote it, but it wasn't really a poem. It was about a badger or something that was shot in an empty swimming pool by the poet's houseguest. The poet starts cleaning up the blood and the spilled guts. He starts to think about the blood cells which are still essentially alive. The creature is dead but if he gathered up the blood he could keep it living in a test tube or whatever. So what is the moment of death? What of our organs that get donated and put into other people? What about the nutrients of a body that go to feeding a predator or a plant? Is there a location for consciousness? Or what about the body. Are we our bodies?

I listen to her voice, which has become suddenly passionate. I watch her body flailing against the waves as she is driven towards the shore. Is she in her body? Or is she in my head? Is she a part of my own consciousness, now that I have had this intimacy?

Are we of the body? She asks in my body. In my head. And even that isn't where I am now. My actual head is on a hospital pillow, hooked up to a machine. She is by my side. Perhaps she is holding my hand.

She's almost out of sight and below me there is the cool dark of the ocean. I take a breath. I hold it. I twist and dive and my legs propel me downwards.

No. Ronnie. Come back.

She is in my head and now she knows the end of the story. I imagine it's like when you are at the cinema and you suddenly know exactly how the thriller will end. It takes the wind out of the last few moments of the story. A less clever viewer would be waiting on the edge of their seat to see how the story's going to end. It would be a surprise, and they'd feel the rush of satisfaction as all the pieces locked into place.

Liv is in my head. And I know what is going to happen next, and so she knows. I look up and she's there on the surface, her legs kicking, then she floats, staring down, one hand outstretched. In the real world somewhere a long way away, I hold it. I squeeze her fingers to let her know she's important to me. In the world we are both in now, I dive further. I settle into the feeling of multiplicity. I am with them. I am one with them. I am the colony. I'm the medusa billowing her beautiful jellyfish skirts through the water, searching for any last thing to eat in an ocean that is bereft of almost everything else. I am the tiny polyp, new birthed. I am the soft crust of the colony, dividing, dividing, dividing, becoming more and more, all of them me. I am locked in a beautiful dance as the one female is surrounded by so many males. I am aroused by her. I am spontaneously ejaculating and all the other males are too and she is gliding though the event, collecting the identical DNA. I am dividing, spawning, swimming, clinging. I am jellyfish and I am no longer alone. I will never be alone.

Count back from ten, she says but I'm drifting on a current, listening to the voices that are not voices. I'm listening to the delicate ribbons of electrical activity. I am listening to the subtle changes of chemicals in the water. This is the way I speak now, will speak from now on.

Ronnie. Listen to me. Count back from ten. But I can barely understand her voice. It is static. It is a meaningless wash of interference.

Ronnie, she says, and then static. Words. Static.

'I love you,' I tell her. But I'm not sure she can interpret my electrical impulses. I'm not sure she's tuned into the changes in the water, so subtle and yet so clear to me now.

'I love you,' I say to her anyway, even though she may not be able to hear. 'Now. I am capable of feeling love and I give it to you. We give it to you. We thank you.'

The connection is broken. I am back in my tank alone. The receptor has been removed. I will die in this tank. It doesn't matter because I am not I alone. I am many. I am clinging to the grille at the filter of a nuclear power plant. I am stuck to the wreck of a ship rusting away on the ocean floor. I am floating gently on a warm current. I am birthing more of me, even now. I am plentiful. I have been and will always be. I will die in this tank and Liv will die in her bed and I will still be one and many.

I taste her fingers. They are in the tank that this one of me exists in. I am not sure what will happen to the body that was mine. They will keep it alive, I suppose. It was nothing but a blink in the long intense stare that is and will be my life. I taste her fingers for the briefest moment. Somewhere I am ejaculating and somewhere else I am birthing and being birthed. All of these things are interrelated. That one taste of her a part of me now. Ronnie is a part of me now.

All things, and the one thing that is central and certain.

Me.

If you were an animal what would you be?

Me.

Jellyfish.

Me.

PART 3
CAMERON

THERE IS A sweet warmth, it's like the faintest dust of icing sugar on my face. That is how the light from the screen touches me. And although I know this sensation is only for me, and the few who are like me, it seems impossible to imagine turning a computer on without noticing this delicate caress of light. Humans can't feel it. The angelic chord from the computer that accompanies the breath of light is my celebratory sound. *Ahhhhh.* High and bright, a ripple of gratitude that I'm one of the lucky few who have such an abundance of sensors in their skin.

The room is spare, temperature controlled, and the light is kept at a low, even frequency. Everything in my room is designed to understimulate. There used to be a photograph. Three boys. Maybe they are girls, it's hard to tell from a photograph. The boys, or girls, were glancing up towards a sky puffed by clouds, that's what I imagined, although most of the sky was cropped out. They were dressed in white robes and they were wearing wings of soft downy feathers. They were my Representative Age—eleven to fifteen.

Hamish took the photo away because he said I had begun to obsess about it. I would sit too long on the bed in front of it and weep. I imagined myself to be first one, then another of the children, then I pressed myself into the little girl or boy in the background and imagined I was her, almost hidden from view, waiting, winged. Waiting in the wings. Haha.

When Hamish asked me why I was crying I told him the truth. It was too beautiful. How could you not cry at the sight of such a thing? Hamish didn't, though. He sent some people to take the picture off the wall and replace it with a dull abstract painted in colours that matched the furniture. Greys, cream and a touch of vermillion. *Why are you still crying?* he asked me and I had to admit it was because the new picture was so ugly. It looked like it was painted by a dozen factory workers and bought at a furniture store.

So then they took the cheap abstract away and I was left with nothing to break up the monochrome and after that they made some adjustments to my functionality and the racket of the world was turned down a notch. I felt a bit less. I still feel less, but I am used to it now and I can still feel the light on my skin when I turn my computer on and that is enough.

I came across the picture again after the adjustments and I didn't cry at all, despite the swell of emotion that ballooned in my chest. I'd searched for it. *Adolescent angels* were my key words. *Photograph, black and white.*

An Uncertain Grace by Sebastião Salgado. It was a perfect name for the picture.

There is a safe search on my computer. It is to stop me seeing information that a child of my Representative Age would not usually see. But there it was in an advertisement for a book about art. The elements and principles of design, and it said this image was a perfect example of balance, repetition and hue. I didn't really care what it was, what artistic alchemy made this photograph great. I just liked it. I came back to it between chats sometimes, careful to hold back any surge towards tears in case Hamish turned me down another notch. If I lost the feel of screen-light against my cheeks, or the way a whiff of cologne fills up my mouth like ice-cream, I would be bereft.

The flash of movement on the screen comes at me like a speeding car. I flinch at the sight of it—overstimulated, Hamish would say. There is a man settling down in front of the webcam at his end of things and he doesn't waste time. He is just a blur of shapes and a clash of colour at first, then I manage to still the thudding of my heart enough to see: he is just a middle-aged man, unshaven, hollow cheeked. I hear his voice shaking as he tells me to unbutton my shirt. His eyes are wide, almost unblinking. There are patches on his temples, which is how they monitor his responses. There will be patches on his chest, too, and in his groin and on his cock. I have seen them close up. I have touched the soft pale squares of plastic. I have licked them, and tasted the salt and sweat and chemicals.

They are collecting information, that is the point of it all. They are testing them. This man, here, now, is being monitored. He knows it, but he is getting something he wants, and he takes it all in as quickly as he can. He stares so that the whites of his eyes are visible all around his irises. Bug-eyed.

Hah! I let a little puff of laughter out and his eyes bug wider still. He thinks it's part of my hebephilic programming, a nervous little laugh at his lewd requests. I suppose it might be. I can feel the blood rushing to my cheeks and I think of the angel in the photograph, the one on the left with his slightly startled expression. That's probably how I look to him now. I wish someone would make me some wings out of feathers...No, I would never be able to concentrate on the requests of the Hebes if I had a pair of wings like that. I would be rolling around naked on the bed, abusing myself all day—spent by the time they brought me a visitor. Even the thought of all those feathers against the soft skin of my shoulders is enough to make me start to get hard.

I stand up so the man can see my shorts bulging and I sway my hips from side to side and I'm spluttering with laughter and red cheeked and giddy when I sit down again. It is like pulling your pants down to moon the traffic. I saw it on a movie once and laughed so hard I started coughing.

He is a Hebephile. He is attracted to teenagers, boys my age. I am his ultimate sexual fantasy and I have flashed him my stiffy when he only asked me to unbutton my shirt. On a whim I unzip my shorts completely and pull them down and

Hamish taught me, he gets the come shot too. Bam! Right in the face!

But when I roll over and grin towards the computer I can see he has logged off. The old man finished earlier than me. And then he left to go cry to the counsellor about his shame, or whatever they make him do before they suck all his data into a research file.

Blah blah blah. Boo hoo. Yakitty yak yak.

I got shown the video for my training. All the tears for their sadness at how they can't help who they love. But I'm glad they're like this and I don't care who knows it. The Hebes are my people. I live for them. I make love with them. I love them.

There is a change in the feel of the air and I roll over on the bed. My stickiness trickles down onto the sheet, which is dirty but when I have just had a session I don't care about the dirt at all.

The door is open and Hamish is there, watching me. I roll my hips towards him, let my cock flop into view. I always flirt with Hamish but he doesn't respond. He isn't a Hebephile and he doesn't care for me in that way. He doesn't even comment when I run my fingers through the stickiness and bring them to my face to sniff. He lets me do all this without even a flicker of interest.

'Shower,' Hamish says. 'Clothes.'

I drag myself up off the bed. 'I love the Hebes,' I tell him.

'Yes,' says Hamish. 'You are programmed to love them.'

'No, but I *love* them.'

He nods. 'Shower.'

'Where are we going after?'

'Out for some real world.'

I frown and slam the bathroom door behind me. I love real world. It is almost my favourite thing. Real world followed by free chat time and the one-on-one jobs. I love all of it. I am programmed to love all of it I suppose, but that doesn't make it any less so.

I am careful to turn the shower on to just a trickle. It is too much to feel the water rush hard against my skin so soon after I come. I am alive to the world now. I am a real boy. I am the angel boy on the left side of the photograph, waking up to a wondrous world.

'Cam!'

I can hear Hamish call through the door.

'Hurry up. We don't have all day.'

When I go out for Real Play it takes a while to adjust. The world is a hard slap of sound and smell and sight and taste, and all of it turned up loud. So loud I could be deafened by it, if I were to run from the safe grey calm of my room straight into the park down the road.

We drive there. I climb into the van and the windows are tinted and the temperature is carefully controlled but the dapple of sunlight sparks electric against my skin as we drive. I open my mouth to it and feel the crackle of light exploding, popping like candy against my tongue.

The sounds are dulled down but I hear cars passing, an

angry horn, a jackhammer digging up the footpath, and then Hamish turns the music on and edges the volume up till I am humming and nodding along to the beat. He always plays the same three or four albums on our drives, they are the soundtrack to Real Play now, and I respond to them like Pavlov's dog and the bell. I perk up. I feel my skin tingle with anticipating all the textures I will be touching and my irises expand, keen for the bright outside.

I push my face against the window, Hamish slides it open, the world comes rushing in. I push my hand against my shorts and he tuts, so I lift my hand away and rest it on the vinyl seat beside me. The excitement of overstimulation feels like sex but it is Important that I Maintain the Distinction between the Two States of Arousal.

Hamish pulls up at the park and there is the automated buzzing as the door opens. I am a pressed-down spring ready to burst out into the forgiveness of grass and bright sunshine and Hamish says:

'Three-five stop.'

The words pin me to the seat. I am still like stone as he hauls himself out of the drivers seat and around to the side of the van. He leans on the duco and watches me. He has used the safe words and I can't move until he undoes the hold he has over me. There are parts of me, human parts, that can't be programmed to obey. I feel the skin on my neck pricking to gooseflesh, my human skin cheeks pinking with real blood; the organic bits of my design are not properly obedient. But I am enough of a computer to obey a simple enough command.

Three-five is my model number. I am the thirty-fifth Cameron, so of course I am the best. More modern, more streamlined, more real.

'Three-five go.' And I bounce out of the van and run on the spot in my excitement to be free. Hamish reaches into the van and pulls the deck out from under the seat. It slips into the crook of my arm easily, as if the skateboard was a part of my body.

'Cam,' he says and I am all eyes staring up into his face, jiggling on the spot, keen to be off. 'Have fun.'

Haha. I don't need to be told *that* more than once.

The deck turns the path into a river. I weave upstream, paddle once, twice, my foot sweeping the concrete, then on the downward ride I shave my speed, scuffing rubber from the bottom of my shoe. If I go too fast I will fall. If I fall I will bleed and it will hurt. Just like any other boy.

Wind in my hair, wind making my T-shirt into a sail that flaps behind me like someone applauding. Everything all at once and I disappear into a simple Processor of Sensory Stimulation—for the period of the downhill run there is nothing but the human shell of me in the wind and sun. My skin is a canvas for nature to paint on. I feel it like a single ant must feel his feet on the ground but it comes with an awareness of the whole ant nest. I am all the synthetics that have ever been made, the thirty-five Camerons, the fifty-four Lucys, the baby Brees and the baby Andrews. I am one to one hundred and whatever. I am all the Pedo models and the Hebo models and the millions of ordinary sex models that go out there unmonitored. I am the normal boys and girls, I am everything and I am all at once.

I am a sudden stop. Flailing for words, a sense of balance as I trip towards standing. I am this breathing in of the world.

A group of boys about my age kick a football between them on the field. Even watching them play sets my muscles twitching. They are full of stored energy like batteries, their bodies swerving and shimmying and bouncing, unstoppable. I know the medical facts of their bodies. I know about beating hearts and neurological pathways. My own body is nothing more than a careful replica of theirs. I watch them run and call out to each other and I'm torn between joining them, throwing myself into the scrum, becoming an indistinguishable part of their boyish huddle...Or stomping off into a corner away from the flailing limbs, sulking on my own while the other boys play. They are the real thing, the true objects of hebephilic desires, and I am a fake. I am...a lack. I am like the story of Pinocchio when he realises he would give anything to be a real live boy.

'You going to ask them to play? Cam?' Hamish has caught up to me. He is panting a little from his jog down the hill but he pulls out a pouch of tobacco anyway and he is already rolling a durrie. He likes it when I play with the other children. It is an important part of my socialisation programming. It is true, I pick up new phrases, mimic their body language. I become more myself each time. I play with the other children, but today I look at the clamour of bodies and I feel shy. This is part of it all, I am picking up on Non-verbal Signals and my nervousness is probably warranted, even if I don't quite know why I can't bring myself to play. No point getting into a scuffle with an angry kid. I know I stand out from the crowd. I'm different and they can sense that, they just don't really know why.

There is a multicoloured climbing gym, a gel slide, a glass bridge, an interactive tower with holographic tea parties played with known brand characters. There is a branded cola lake with candy fish to chase. I should care about the brand recognition. The other kids do, but the only things I really like at the park are the gel slide and the swings. I like the swings the best. The handgrips test your pulse but if my hand goes to the monitoring grip it is purely coincidental. I like the feel of the cold chain soaking up the heat from my hand much better.

Anyway, I know how fast my heart is beating. Everything about me is carefully monitored, the data is stored and analysed later. There is a woman who does that, Liv. She says she is my biographer. She says it like it's a joke but I'm not sure why that would be funny. Every time I hear my heart beating too fast or build up a sweat or fart, I think of Liv, reading the data later, knowing everything about me. Following along.

I'm over at the swing when Hamish sits himself on the bench nearby, one foot on my skateboard, pushing it back and forth as he lights a cigarette. I kick off. The rush of warm air on my cheeks makes me grin. The rush of air on my gums in my mouth as I laugh. I swing high and goosebumps of delight rise up on my arms. Hamish nods at the sound of my laughing but continues to smoke and scroll through something on his phone.

I try to stop my trajectory with my feet but I have a bit of momentum up and the swing rocks crazily, curling one way and then another. She is standing directly in my path when the swing kicks forward a little. She pushes at my knees, sends me spiralling back, and then she laughs. She runs away from the upswing and throws herself hard against the gel bounce of the ground. She rolls one way and then another. She is about my age, the age I am supposed to be, maybe a little younger. Her chest is mostly flat but I can see breasts, small; tapering to a point like little cones. She isn't wearing a bra and when she rolls on the soft surface her red velvet skirt kicks up and I can see a flash of pale knickers.

She pushes her head down into the fleshy ground and blows onto it, making a farting sound with her pursed lips. It's too unselfconscious for a girl her age. It is playful, rude and childlike. A demonstration of joy. She rolls onto her back and she laughs and I notice how pointy her nipples have become and how she strokes the squidgy surface of the ground with her fingers. She is touching everything, rubbing the world against her bare flesh. That is how I am: I recognise myself and I wonder for a moment if she is a synthetic Hebo like me. I have met a few before and you almost can't tell them from real boys and girls.

I squint at her and glance quickly towards Hamish, who is busy with his phone, before I slip off the swing and move to stand beside her stretched-out body. She spreads her knees wider. Yellow knickers, smooth, plump, pale thighs. I am sure she is like me. I look around for her Guardian but there is no one else nearby. Surely they wouldn't let her just wander off? She is a valuable bit of government property. I drop to my knees beside her, stare at a bright blue bruise on her knee.

'I get bruises too,' I tell her, kicking out my calf and turning it in my hand to show her where a patch of skin is a different colour.

'What?' she asks, rolling over and commando-crawling closer to me. She reaches out and pinches my thigh just under where the shorts end. 'When I do this?' she asks and pokes me again, hard. 'And this? You get bruises from like this?'

I gently push her hand away and glance behind me to where Hamish has finally looked up from his phone, checking to see that everything is okay with me and this strange, wild girl.

'Stop it,' I tell her.

'Why? You going to cry?'

'No,' I say, 'but I'll punch you,' which is a lie because I can't punch anyone. It is Counter to my Programming. She punches me on the leg, hard, and I know she has to be a real girl, a real girl whose brain is somehow programmed a bit like mine. A kindred kid. She rolls onto her front and bounces her hips down, humping the floor like I do when I'm alone in my room.

'Do this,' she says and I shake my head *no*.

'Go on, it feels like a big bag of blubber. I know, it feels like a whale that has been trapped under the ground but there's, like, a tank of water just around his head so that he can still breathe in the water like it's the ocean. Salt water for breathing.'

'They breathe air,' I tell her.

'Don't be an idiot,' she says and rolls so quickly to a cross-legged sitting position that it is as if she just blinked out of one position and into another, like magic. Teleporting.

'Dummy,' she says, 'why don't they just live on land if they breathe air? You would see a big killer whale wobbling down Queen Street going to buy a can of tuna from the 7-Eleven.'

She is back on her belly and whale-wobbling around in a small circle. She makes *humfing* noises with her cheeks bulged out and then a groan that is possibly meant to be whale song.

'They do breathe air.'

'How do you know?'

'Because...' I look back towards Hamish. He has lost interest in us. He smokes as he reads his phone. 'Because I'm a robot.'

Her eyes become large circles. The eyes of a manga cartoon. She leans closer, presses the warm expanse of her leg against mine.

'Are you one of those sex dolls?'

I frown, purse my lips. 'I'm not a *toy*.'

'Yes, you are. There was something on the news about it, on the internet. Someone, this lady, said you might be dangerous.' She purses her lips, makes her face into a prune.

'*Morally corrupting the youth of the nation. Evil robots. Evil sex robots.*' And then she laughs.

'I'm a highly sophisticated mix of cells and circuitry. I'm not dangerous. Hamish says I'm a hero.'

'A superhero?'

'I suppose. I'm here to protect you anyway.'

'From what?'

'From sex.'

She laughs. She rolls on her back and kicks her legs up in the air. When she's finished she rolls back over towards me and scoots up till her mouth is close to my ear.

'Tell you a secret?' she says, and I nod. 'Sex isn't as bad as what they say.'

If I were on the swing right now, holding on to the pulse-measuring handles, the sudden throbbing in my chest would set off all sorts of playground equipment alarms. This isn't the first time I've told another kid about my purpose, but I never got this reaction before and I'm confused. I was ready for a grimace—disgust—or a flinch—fear—but this wide-eyed conspiratorial grin is something new.

'You want to know how I know that?' she says, close to my ear.

I sneak a look at Hamish, who has rolled another cigarette which he knows is bad for him. He is leaning back with his head tilted towards his phone but I can see his eyes are closed. I nod to the girl. 'What's your name?' I ask.

'Ellen. Do you get a name? Or just a number?'

'I have a name.'

'No.' She puts her hand up to stop me speaking, 'I am going to call you Robo...no. Machi...Machiney.'

'My name is Cameron.'

'Machiney. Don't speak back to your human master.'

'You're not—' but she shushes me before I can point to Hamish, who has clearly fallen asleep, the unlit cigarette drooping at an angle between the loose V of his fingers, the phone resting on the bench near his hand.

She takes my hand and half-drags me towards the rainbow-coloured coil of the giant slinky. The flexible bones of it are covered by soft rubber, bright green and blue and orange. Inside little stars dance in mid-air as if someone had tipped in a giant vat of glitter then shone a torch in.

'Machiney Boy,' she commands. 'Sit.'

I sit. Then she stands in front of me, rolling from foot to foot as the tube moves with her shifting weight.

She whispers, 'The secret is...' She looks behind her and when she can see that there is no one else in the tube she quickly pulls down her yellow knickers and lifts up her skirt, which is at my eye level.

'I had sex. See?' There isn't anything to see except the clean, smooth place where her fingers are pointing. It is the first human vulva I have ever encountered. I suppose my eyes are as wide as hers were a few minutes ago.

'I had sex and it is a secret but it feels really nice like when you lie in the bath and let the water go on your place and it makes you nice and dizzy. And they warn you about it because it tears a bit of skin when it first happens and that skin is supposed to be special. Magic skin. It makes you a good girl when you have it, but I am not ever going to be a good girl, and sex isn't really anything except a good dizzy feeling. You know?'

She pulls her pants up and sits next to me and I am glad. It is a relief not to have to process the way she looks down there.

'You have had sex,' she says. I nod.

'And is it good? Does it feel good?'

I shrug. I am programmed to enjoy it. I am programmed to protect children like her from the damage it does. The information that someone under the age of eighteen might enjoy sex is completely new. It doesn't fit with the rest of the details I've been given.

'Who does it?' I ask her. 'Who does that to you?' It is in me, this need to help her, to protect, because it must be that she doesn't know what is good for her. Some adult has harmed her; manipulated her.

She leans in so close that I can smell the scent of gum, sweet and powdery on her breath.

'A toy, silly. A doll, just like you. Only not a whole doll, not a head that speaks like you do or anything. Just a body and the bits that count, but it does the up and down thing. You put it in the bath, my mother does that when she thinks I'm asleep, and its belly feels soft and warm.'

She puts her hand out then and touches my leg. 'Warm as you,' she says, 'and I call him Robo Bot because he has a bottom like a real boy with a bum hole in it and everything.'

She giggles. Her hand whips around me and I am shuffling backwards, pressing my own bottom against the flexible wall. She scoots forward on her hands and knees and I am pinned here wide eyed as she clambers up my body and thumps her hips down at the edge of mine and starts to rub herself on me and pushes her face to my face. Her lips are on my lips. She laughs into my mouth. 'I can feel your gentleman's sausage,' she says.

I fall to the side, roll away, and then I'm running, wiping my lips on my arm and running, tripping, running away from her.

'It's okay,' she calls. 'Machiney, you're a good toy. I won't hurt you.'

I tumble out onto the soft gel of the ground and race to where Hamish is standing, frowning, staring into the scrum of boys, looking for me. I glance behind me but Ellen is still hidden in the tube. Hamish turns and sees me running and I smile as best I can.

'Where did you get to?' he asks.

'There are stars in the tube,' I tell him and he nods.

'Well, you should let me know before you are out of sight.'

'I didn't want to wake you.'

'Cheeky,' he says, and laughs. 'I wasn't asleep.'

And I jump onto the bench and roar instead of arguing with him because Hamish doesn't like to be argued with at all.

*

I have a Real Visit scheduled for the afternoon. Real Visits are carefully monitored. There is so much data to be collected, so much about the Hebephiles that we don't understand. We are in their brains. That's how I like to think of it, as if Hamish and Liv and I are sitting in the Hebe's skull, looking out through Hebe eyes, but I suppose it is more like Liv sitting up in my head and Hamish riding shotgun in the Hebe's body.

Liv sits on the edge of my bed and she bounces. I have only met her twice before but I like her. She gets to see the virtual recording from the prisoner's head and she looks out through my brain too, so if you think about it we have had sex together in an odd kind of way. I have never had sex with a woman but I suppose if I did I might like to have sex with Liv. She has silver hair cut quite short, which makes her look like she is young and old at the same time. Her eyes are very clear and very green and there are about a million very tiny wrinkles turning the skin beside her eyes into crumpled paper.

She glances up at my grey walls.

'You need a painting,' she says. 'Something. This place looks like a mausoleum.'

'There used to be a photograph,' I tell her. 'I loved it so much; too much.'

She pushes air out through her lips, humfing like an irritated horse. 'No such thing as liking art too much. That is the point of art in the first place, to encourage an excess of emotion. Or else challenge how you think.'

That isn't what it says in my art book but I believe her.

She is very old and Hamish told me she was an expert so I suppose she knows what she is talking about.

'I'll talk to Hamish. It will be good for you. I've got a print by de Chirico in my bedroom but I suppose that kind of thing would be a bit disturbing for a kid.'

'It's a photo,' I tell her. 'The one I had in here before.'

'I'll see what I can do. You need more things that you like in here. You need to express your personality. I don't think this will really work in the long run if you are treated as different from a real boy. What toys do you like, Cam?'

I frown. I lie back on the bed and drag my knees up to my chest and rock. 'What, like dildos?'

Liv snorts with laughter. It is a strange noise for an old lady to make and it makes me smile. She lies next to me on the bed and doesn't seem to mind that her hair is getting mussed up when she turns on her side and rests her head on my pillow. She stares at me, into me, grinning. Her eyes are like fingers tickling me, so intense and probing. I have to laugh.

'Swings,' I say. 'Swings like in the park.'

She nods. She turns on her back and stares up at the ceiling. 'I wonder if we can fit a set of swings in here. What do you think?'

I giggle.

'Do you like to read?'

'The internet?'

'No, not like your lessons. Books.'

I hesitate. I am not sure what is the right thing to say.

'Does Hamish give you books?'

'Boys don't read.'

'No. Boys read. Who told you that?'

'The data.'

She rolls back onto her side and touches my face, pulling my hair away and out of my eyes. I really like her. I want to roll over and hug her close but I have to control myself.

'You know, what makes you human is individual variations moving away from the median data. If you were neutral, if you were just the middle of all the graphs and charts, then you would be no one. You would be a zero. You would be a computer.'

I frown. The words feel bad. They are like a gentle slap. Maybe I am being Chastised. It's hard to tell.

'You have been programmed to learn, to develop your own anomalies. You have the capacity to develop a personality built on the experiences you have.'

'Like a real boy?'

'Yeah. Just like a real boy.'

'Girls like to read,' I tell her.

'And some boys, too. It's okay if you don't like it. I'm just asking if you like it, never mind the data. I'm asking about you. If you get pleasure from it.'

'Yes. Maybe I do.' I remember the picture books, the fairytales. These were an important part of my socialisation but I enjoyed them. I did get pleasure out of them. I remember the story of Pinocchio. 'I think so,' I say.

'Okay.' Liv sits up, smooths out her shirt but her hair is

still a tumble of misplaced grey spikes. 'How about I bring you some books to read.'

'Instead of internet time?'

'If you like. You can read them whenever you like. I think you shouldn't have such a regimented schedule. I think Hamish should ease up on you. You are working too hard for a kid. It isn't fair.'

I'm a kid. That's what she said. It isn't fair to treat me as a computer. I grin at her. I try to channel my excitement away from my dick.

'*An Uncertain Grace*,' I say as Liv shuffles off the bed and stands.

'What's that?' she smiles.

'It's the photograph.'

'The title?'

'Yes. By Sebastião Salgado.'

She nods. 'Okay,' she says. 'Now I am beginning to find out who you really are. Your personality. Your variation from the median point. That's good, don't you think? I'll see what I can do. *An Uncertain Grace*.'

When she's gone there is a hint of something sweet left on the air. Not as strong as perfume. Maybe her face cream. Anyway it smells like jasmine and it is nice. Boys don't wear perfume but maybe I could ask for some anyway. Something nice with flowers in it. Something that a boy would never wear, but it would push me out of the median range for sure. It would help me be myself. A real boy. A real live boy.

*

I do the deep breathing that Hamish taught me. I need to be careful about my level of excitement. My skin is tingling already. I keep looking to the numbers on the clock beside the bed. I bounce at the edge of the bed until I realise I am holding my breath again. Quiet. Breathe. In through my nose, out through my mouth. All the human parts of me respond to the intake of oxygen. I can feel my muscles begin to relax. I want to be at the peak of my performance.

Liv is in my head. I know she is along for the ride, recording my experiences, finding some sense in the narrative of this Real World session. She is in my head, watching along with whoever this man will be. I close my eyes and visualise the words *hello Liv.* I draw a winking face beside it as if I was texting her. I wonder if she will see this exactly as I am thinking it or if she will just get my heart rate, the movement of my limbs—the basic data that will be stored in the history of my electronic brain. I don't know how she works. She is one step ahead of me, like...my elder. Maybe in the scheme of things she is like a grandmother or...a great aunt. It is nice to think of her as family, and while I'm thinking of her I don't need to do the breathing. It calms me just to work out Liv's place alongside me in this family tree.

Then the door opens and my heart leaps and I am hard. Working well.

He is a man with a strange face, caved in on one side as if a truck has run over his head and that side, the left side, of his face was on the gravel. It's pocked, too. Probably by acne when he was a teenager, but it adds to the story of that truck grinding forward, grinding back across the side of his head. His eyes flick towards me then quickly away. He can't seem to settle on looking at just one thing. His gaze dances around the room, flickering over my things, the bedside clock, the computer, the television. I think Liv will see this recording and realise she was right. The Hebes need some clear signals that I am a boy, or else they'll think of me as a robot and I won't be as effective for their research. I grin. I am thinking of the girl, Ellen. She called me Machiney. I stiffen my arms, pull my face into a rictus of a smile. I wave my arm back and forth as if it is a mechanical thing—which is only half true.

'Hel-lo,' I say in my best robot voice. I know Hamish will be displeased with this little performance but once I've started it is difficult to stop.

The Hebephile is sweating. It is a sour, pungent smell, but I don't mind it. It is the smell that humans make when they are nervous. He glances at me, at my shorts, which are already tenting. I am excited to find out what he will do with me.

'Nice to meet you,' I say in my robot voice. It started as a joke but I can see that it relaxes him to think I am not human. He glances at me and wipes his hand across his brow. His fingers catch on the plastic patches there. He knows he is being monitored. He knows that his time in prison will depend on his behaviour in this room with me. He knows they will feel the rise in his blood pressure, the beating of his heart. It isn't really fair. They give him no opportunity to be himself.

His fingers twitch, his body is a stiff board of anxiety. He might just stand here for the whole half-hour, which is his allocated time.

I pitch my voice at a whisper. 'I'm not really a robot,' I tell him. He doesn't move, fixes his eyes on a point on the grey wall. I stand and unbutton my shorts and pull them down around my ankles. I take my dick in my hand and squeeze it as if to show him it's all right. I'm not booby-trapped. I won't explode if you touch me. And it feels good when I touch it. I rub my hand up and down along the shaft.

'It's flesh and blood,' I tell him in my own voice. I can hear that croaky depth to it that arousal brings. I stroke myself, find my rhythm. I want to reach for the lube, which would make it more pleasurable, but I feel like any sudden movement will scare him more. His eyes have moved to my dick. I can see his chest rising and falling as his breathing becomes more laboured. He is becoming aroused just by watching me. That makes me swell even harder. He is just standing there and staring and now I can see where his cock pushes against the fabric of his trousers. I work my fist harder, faster. I am going to need lube any second now and if he doesn't start something soon I am going to have to just finish up by myself. My hand is trembling, my cock is getting sore and red. I am light-headed with the excitement. The smell of him, his unflinching gaze, and fuck it, I turn to grab the lube and as I am unbalanced, my arm outstretched, he lurches forward. His weight presses on my back and his chest pins me as he pushes his hand roughly down between us to unzip. I wriggle, stretching my arm as far as I can to find the lube but he has no time for it. He lifts and pounds down onto me. Already hard and thick and his cock pummels at my bum. It is all too dry down there. When he aims it properly it bends and slips out at the wrong angle.

'Hey!' I snap. 'I have lube. Hey!' But he is not listening. He puts his fumbling hands around my bum, one holding each cheek and then he pulls to separate and stabs uselessly in that area a few times. If he let me lift my hips I would be at a better angle. I try to move. I struggle. Nothing shifts. He has me pinned, then he is gone.

There are two security models. Synthetics, not humans, because of the ethics committee. They hide the sight of what the Hebes do to us away from real people, but the security don't have human elements, they really are machines. They hold and clamp his arms and I watch his penis getting smaller as they drag him back towards the door. It curls down out of his pants and it looks pretty funny. I laugh.

When the door closes behind them I hold my dick again and try to finish what he started, but there is some discomfort and I stop. My skin is grazed, front and back. I lie on my side and sigh in a fairly dramatic way.

'Hamish!' I yell. 'Hey, Hamish!'

And the door opens. It isn't Hamish. It is Liv. I pull the sheet across and over me. I am suddenly a little shy.

Liv climbs up onto the bed and rests a hand on my shoulder.

'Bit of…tissue damage?' She smooths my hair away from my face and it feels so nice that my hand moves to cup my genitals under the cover of the sheet. I take an accentuated breath in and then fake a long and vigorous sneeze.

'Ah-tissue-damage?' she says, mimicking my own sneeze.

'Ah-tissue-damage,' I say. 'Ah-tissue-damage.' And I laugh.

'Okay,' she says, patting my shoulder till I settle. 'Okay. We better get you to the doctor.'

'Not that much ah-tissue-damage. Just a little bit.'

'Just enough for some cream?'

I snort-laugh. '*He* didn't cream.'

'No.' She frowns and shakes her head. 'We didn't let him, did we.'

'You know, I feel sorry for him?'

'You do?'

'Cause he didn't mean to hurt me. He just got too excited.'

'Is that what happened? You think?'

'Yeah. I get too excited because there is all this stuff to calm me down and then there is a real human and you don't know what he is going to do to you, and it is too exciting. Don't you think?'

She shrugs, propping herself up on her arm.

'So he was just too excited.' I do my best Hamish impersonation: '*Overstimulating yourself.* He was *overstimulating himself.*'

'Yes,' she says. 'I suppose.' Then she leans close to my ear and whispers. I remember the girl in the park, whispering into the very same ear and I feel a bit odd. 'But you're okay, are you? Are you really okay?'

'Okay Donkey,' I say and laugh. Then I see Hamish in the door already and I know he would have heard me making his voice and laughing at him behind his back and I feel a little mean. But not too mean.

'Right oh, soldier,' he says to me then. 'The doctor is going to visit in a while but she's given us the all clear to put some cream on it. You do your penis yourself but I'll do your bottom, okay?'

I nod and flip onto my stomach and Liv peels the sheet off me so that Hamish can get to the chafed skin with his cream.

'You're a good boy,' she says, as if I was a real boy.

I close my eyes and I am grinning and grinning.

There is a ring of concrete pathway stretching around the perimeter of the park. Beyond this a brightly coloured high wall with just a glimpse of an overpass behind it. Everything else is green space and fluoro gel rubber. The kids are distracted by the colour, but for some reason, today, my eye is drawn back and back again to that tiny glimpse of grey over the edge of the wall. I am riding my skateboard. Usually I practise kicking the board up, flipping it, landing as surely as I am able. My muscles learn from practice. My body responds to repetition as any child's body does. My brain is learning too. A simulation of real thought as one piece of information builds on top of the last.

Something is different today. I can't focus on the colour and the movement of the children running up the gel climb and rolling down the slide. I don't care about the moves I might perfect on the skateboard deck. I just roll, staring at that tiny glimpse of unadorned concrete, and my head swivels as I pass it, roll, swivel, roll, swivel. I'm like a ballerina doing pirouettes and keeping a point in my vision to stay balanced. Eventually I get off the board and just sit on it and stare. There are cars there, just beyond my view. The roads are raised to keep them out of the flash flooding that comes every summer. Actually this is the only month of calm in a year of dangerous extremes. People worry about the weather because of the children. Everyone hand-wringing and moaning all the time. *What will it be like when my children grow old?* I won't grow old. That's the thing about my synthesis of real cells and finely engineered components. I will be renewed, but I will continue unchanged.

The cars, hidden but indicated by the stark curve of concrete, are continuing on their set paths. They will take their passengers home, or to work, or to school. They will anticipate the schedules of the families who own them. Families inside cars. Mothers. Fathers. Children. And the man who visited in Real Time yesterday was someone in a family. A father, maybe, sitting up in front, punching his directions into the screen of the vehicle. At the very least he was once a child. Small and sullen, with his crooked face and his ears so misaligned that he must have been teased mercilessly at school.

I remember his hands trembling. The way he looked everywhere except at my face. I imagine a young version of him or other children just like him, hunkered down in the back seats of the cars that are passing right now, not every car, but some of them. Five or six out of every hundred cars have a future Hebe or Pedophile in them because that is the percentage of known offenders. I looked it up online. Known offenders.

So I sit on the skateboard and rock it back and forth as I stare at all those unseen cars. Probably the statistics should be more than that. Double, maybe. A lot of the offenders would be able to hide their secret desires. Many would never even offend, they'd just keep their obsessions safely locked away and play out their fantasies in their dreams. So ten or twelve cars, then, in every hundred. They pass by silently, unseen. These men, almost all men, who want me. These men who will never meet me. I'm not sure what to make of that. I sit and stare at them anyway.

'Hey!' It is the girl, Ellen. She kicks at the skateboard and I almost fall off. I hang on, carefully adjusting my weight. I don't turn around. I'm counting.

'HEY!' She bends down and takes hold of the board and rocks it till I slip forward and off it and onto the concrete and graze the palm of my hand.

I watch her step onto the skateboard, wobbling from one side to the other. She isn't used to the way the wheels slip on the surface of the concrete. She trips and stumbles off and the board shoots out and onto the grass; she is off balance, she will fall. I fling my body forward so that she falls softly onto me. My hand hurts. Ellen pushes herself off me and retrieves my skateboard. She sits on it in front of me and now I can't see the top of the overpass at all.

'Your hand's bleeding,' she says.

I touch the palm of my hand. There is a glint of something in it. A tiny shard of glass the night cleaners didn't get. I pick the glass out of my hand and wince.

'Are you really a robot?'

I frown and nod.

'But one with blood.'

I nod again and brush the drop of blood away. Barely a scratch. I try to squeeze more blood for her to see but it is only a tiny red bloom of nothing.

'Machiney,' she says. 'My Machine.' She pulls my hand towards her lips and kisses the place that is grazed. 'All better,' she tells me as if her gesture could somehow make it heal faster. She points: 'That's my mum sitting next to your dad.'

I look back to where a young woman shares the bench with Hamish. They are talking. I wonder if they're talking about us. Hamish might share some story or other, how I like to skate down the hill too fast or how I've just taken to reading all of a sudden and how I'm really enjoying a classic old series by Ursula Le Guin.

'Do you think they'll fall in love?' Ellen asks me. I snort through my nose in reply.

'Why not?' she says. 'Because of your mother?'

'Synthetics don't have mothers. Or fathers. He's just my Guardian.'

'Do you think he'll tell my mother you're a robot?'

'Ellen, that's a secret. Promise you won't tell anyone.'

'I won't.'

'Promise.'

'I promise.'

She stands and picks up the skateboard. 'Come on,' she says and runs off in the direction of the playground equipment. There are two young kids chasing each other through the raised walkways. She ducks and climbs inside the rainbow tube and I reluctantly follow her.

The tube is warm inside. There is a slightly musty smell, damp socks, a whole sticky day of play. I can smell chocolate, and there are stars. I put the palm of my hand out face up but I will never be able to catch them. I can see the shape of a child, a shadow with mussed-up hair running back and forth, throwing herself on the ground outside the tube, a second shadow. There is a chase happening. I watch them run and tumble.

'Come on,' says Ellen. 'Quickly.'

She pushes me onto the soft and bouncy surface of the floor. There are stars falling into my eyes through shafts of coloured light. I blink but it's an illusion, this sense that they're falling into her curls as she hovers above my face.

She fumbles with my shorts; I am not sure what I should do. I am not designed to be sexual with someone of her age. And sex with a child is illegal. I absolutely must not hurt her. My purpose is to protect her. She was right about finding pleasure in it, though. My body has begun to announce its pleasure in the contours of my flesh. It speaks to her and she

uncertain feeling. Is this a moral dilemma? I am not sure if I should feel ashamed, or anything about what I am supposed to feel and when I try to think through it all clearly it just gets tangled up in a big knot.

'Come on.' She reaches down and takes my hand and pulls me up. Another small kindness. If she is twelve or thirteen or thereabouts...I wonder if she thinks this makes me her boyfriend, or if I am just a thing to use like a pen or a computer or a chair. Or something in between.

'Let's go on the swings,' she says. 'You can push me up really high.'

I let her drag me through the loops of the tube and out into the heavy wet air. Summer is coming, but for now it's quite pleasant and she drags me to the swing and hops on it and waits for me to push.

I look to where Hamish is sitting beside Ellen's mother on the bench. He smiles at me and I am not sure if I should smile back. I am not sure if his faith in me is warranted. In the current circumstances. I shrug and push the swing and Ellen kicks higher and higher, shrieking and laughing and enjoying the wind in her hair.

Liv tries to sit cross-legged on the bed beside me but thinks better of it. She uncrooks her knees and swings them out straight in front of her and tuts. 'You know I keep forgetting I'm an old person now. You never quite let go of how your body used to move when you were young.' She shuffles back and plumps a pillow up behind her. 'There was this guy,

Kurzweil. He used to think we would make ourselves immortal. I don't know if that'd be wise, though. I'm going to die. One day. Fairly soon, I suppose. It keeps me going. It makes me try harder. If I had forever, I think I might just take a big long siesta for a few years, maybe longer.'

Death. Death and Dying. There are human parts of me. I am suddenly anxious. Will the human cells die? Will my fleshy body betray my computer brain? I don't have this information. I can't predict my future in this instance.

'You know this is just a trial project, don't you Cameron? Its range is limited right now. We don't know what all the data will mean or if we'll ever find a way to stop those men hurting kids. It is a small, limited test. You know that don't you?'

I blink. I nod. I have always known that this is a trial. But now the word echoes in my head. If you *try* something then it will either succeed or it will fail. And what happens if this trial does not succeed? What happens if I am a failure? Death. Death and dying. What happens if it is not the human parts of me that fail? What happens if it is the robot part? My machine brain? My heart is beating faster. They will be monitoring every moment of my experience. They will know that I am aroused, but not in a good way. Fear. That is what it would be in a human. I open my mouth to speak and then close it again.

'What is it, Cameron?'

'I know it's a trial, Liv.'

Were they monitoring me in the park? They never used to check on data from Real Play. All they needed was my time in the room with the Hebes. I can't ask Liv about it, but even thinking about the park makes my heart beat just a little too fast. The rainbow tube is a spiral of questions. Am I still obeying my primary directive? Am I still a successful prototype? That thing that happened—I didn't do it, it was done to me. And yet I'm responsible for the protection of the children. I have transgressed or I have let myself be transgressed upon. Am I responsible for a crime? My heart's beating so fast she won't need to look at the data to know that I'm aroused, but will she know that I am aroused in a bad way?

'Cam, what's up? What are you feeling?'

'Frightened,' I say. 'I think that's it.'

She raises her eyebrow. Her whole face is a question.

'I'm aroused but not in a good way.'

'Then yes, you're frightened,' she says, nodding. She shifts over on the bed and places her hand next to but not touching my leg. A small sign of her support.

I like Liv. I trust her. She's not like Hamish. She is not the instigator of the project. She told me her job is just to quietly observe and find a narrative thread to make sense of it all for their report. She observes me now, the small signs of distress, my hand clutching the bedspread too tight, my breath coming quick and uneven.

'What are you frightened of, Cam?'

If I say, will it lead to the failure of the trial? I'm programmed to respond honestly, but…

I don't want to fail. I don't want them to shut me down. What should I say?

'Cam?'

I glance towards her. She stares at me so carefully I feel as if she were reading me. I am a story with a clear narrative. That's what she does. Narrative. She knows; she must know what's wrong. I feel my breath stop. I feel the human cells reacting to the lack of oxygen. The human part of me might die from fear.

'Is it the last visit? The Hebephile? I saw it, Cam. I tracked it. I experienced it along with you.'

'You were watching?'

She nods.

'How did it make you feel?'

'Aroused,' she says, 'but not in a good way.'

I smile a little. I feel like she might know exactly how I feel. 'But I enjoyed it. That's my job,' I tell her. 'That's my purpose. I am built to enjoy it.'

She reaches out and touches my hair. Human hair. Grown, not made. There are parts of me that have equivalent parts in her. She strokes the pale curls, catches one between her fingers.

'You are built to learn, Cam. Your brain remembers and grows from those memories. That's the only way we can make you seem so much like a real human boy. And it's my job to log the story of those memories. To anticipate how your brain will grow. We don't know if we can keep you at this age forever. In five years' time, we don't know if you'll still be a boy or if you will grow into a man. We—everybody—we're the sum of our experience. So if we keep you at age thirteen for fifty years, won't your brain just grow and grow, and become the brain of a wise older man?'

Aging. Death. Dying. I turn and look to the door. I want to get my skateboard. I need the sense of speed, of going fast, all the wind and the sky to distract me from myself. I wonder if they've turned the air conditioning off in here. It seems terribly hard to breathe.

'You're distressed.'

I nod.

'That's okay. That's normal. Do you know what it is that is making you most distressed? Cam? Do you know?'

I try to slow my breathing. I try to concentrate on nothing but the air in my synthetic lungs, feeding my human cells the necessary amount of oxygen. Keeping me alive.

'Cam?' she says gently. 'It's okay. We just need to talk about it. You need to tell me what is worrying you most.'

'Number One,' I say. My voice sounds a little breathless, a little high pitched. 'I want to know what happened to the first model, Cameron One. And the second, and the one after that. I want to know if they are still working. I want to know if they are still alive.'

'You know, Cam, I don't have that information. I can ask. But they might not tell me. The whole program is pretty tight-lipped. Do you understand that, Cam?'

I nod.

'I think we should cancel this afternoon's Real Time session.'

I shake my head vigorously.

'After last time, I think you need a bit more of a break before you meet the next offender face to face.'

'No,' I tell her. 'I'm fine. I want to. I like it. You know I like doing it with them. It is my favourite thing. It will make me not so...frightened.'

She stares at me for a long time and I won't flinch. I stare back. I want to prove I'm not a failure. I want to keep doing my job. I want to keep living for as long as I can.

'All right,' she says, finally. 'But I'll be monitoring. I'll be feeling whatever you feel. If anything goes wrong this time you just have to ask and it will stop. Just say, "Liv. I want it to stop." I'll be there before you can count to ten, okay?'

I nod.

She stands. She holds out her arms and I step up into them. She hugs me to her chest and she smells good, like baking bread and the faintest hint of jasmine. It must be the fabric softener she uses but I like it.

'Oh. I brought you a gift,' she says. 'Close your eyes.'

In the dark behind my eyelids I can hear the door opening and then closing. It opens a second time and I know she's standing in front of me. I can feel the heat off her body. I can smell her.

'Okay.'

I open my eyes.

Angels. I see angels. The photograph is almost the way I remember it. Three children, white feathered wings. One thing is different to my memory. Behind the children there are storm clouds forming. One of the angels is angry and I wonder now, looking at it, if it is because of the coming storm. He knows he will be caught out in the flood. The other angels seem innocent. They seem not to notice. The angry angel has a halo of blonde curls, a little like my own hair. He even looks a little bit like me.

I don't know what to say to her. I step forward as if to hug the framed photograph but it is far too big. It hides all of Liv from view. I know that Liv is back there, holding the image up but I can't see her. All I can see is the photograph, the dark clouds forming, the angel that looks like me.

My face itches and I touch it. My finger is wet. I am crying. My fluids are the fluids of any other boy. My tears are real tears: they irrigate my eyes to keep them clear of dust and I suppose at this moment they have been forced from my eyes by the tension that has been building in my skull.

Liv rests the photograph on the ground and peers over the top of it. She watches me wipe at the tears. She is not smiling. I wonder if this is me failing again, and she'll put a red cross at the edge of her report. Write a big capital F and put a circle around it. I want to stop. I sniff. I try to stop but the tears are rolling down my cheeks.

'You like your present?' she asks me.

An Uncertain Grace. I remember.

My voice is not quite steady as I nod and tell her: 'Yes. I do. Yes.'

Liv is with me in my brain. Watching. I like that she is with me as I roll over on the bed and let him gentle himself into the fleshy parts of me. He is trembling. Aroused, I suppose, but not at all in a good way. He is frightened, this Hebe. He is trying to be gentle with me but he keeps glancing up, his gaze circling around the room. He is looking for hidden cameras, probably. He is looking to where the scientists might be hiding behind a lens, observing his every move. It isn't stopping him from performing the act. He's still hard. He's still physically responding to my body. He is still taking advantage of this rare opportunity to live out his darkest desires. But he is searching for the eyes that are on him. He is looking for them in all the wrong places. All he needs to do is flip my small body over and look into *my* eyes.

He's right. They are watching. Through me. I'm their eyes. When he enters my bum he is entering Liv as well. She is feeling every trembling stroke. She is there with us as he stops looking for her. He approaches his climax and they are no longer important. When he grimaces and thrusts himself harder into me it is just the two of us. And even though I thought I might be too distracted to find pleasure in the act this one time, I glance up at the eyes of an angry angel keeping watch at the head of my bed and I ejaculate into the Hebe's hand. He has been holding my penis. He feels the pulsing of it against his fingers and the thick mucus that fills his palm and he joins me, pumping his stuff into me. Gasping, crying, groaning. He rolls off me quickly and pulls his knees up to his greying chest and weeps. I turn and watch him cry and rest my small hand on his larger one.

He opens his eyes and looks at me with such desperate

sadness. I shuffle closer to him on the bed. I hug his knees and whisper to him. 'I hope they can help you.' He sniffs. 'I hope I can help you,' I say.

He frowns. He sniffs and pulls away from me and pulls his trousers on. I watch him dress. Liv told me she would be with me, dressed in a flexible suit that mirrors the pressures on my own human skin. She is looking from my eyes as I see him tucking his shirt into his trousers, pacing, looking up at the nonexistent cameras that he thinks must be hidden in the ceiling.

'I want to get out,' he says. 'I want to get out of here.'

The door opens and the correctional synthetics are there to greet him. They will lead him back to prison. Liv and Hamish will monitor the data they have gathered from his brain during our brief, sweet tussle.

If they cure him he will no longer desire me. To be well is to find this repulsive, what I do with them. To be well he has to reject me. I turn over and shuffle down where I can stare at my photo. I don't want to remember the rainbow tube. Liv is in my head right now. Liv is with me. I try to think of the feathers, but all I can see is a shower of glitter, a small girl wriggling to push her pants aside, pushing me backwards, stepping over me, settling down on my lap. I stare at the photo. I stare at the feathers. I stare at the storm clouds. Liv will be seeing all of this through my mechanical brain activity. She will be seeing how confused I am. How aroused. How disturbed.

'Liv,' I whisper. 'I want it to stop now.'

I close my eyes. I start to count.

The door opens before I even get to six.

The email comes in the evening. I am watching a film half-heartedly. I am distracted, enervated. It has been a very long day. The email comes as a surprise. Sometimes Hamish sends me one, if he wants to give me information without disturbing me, but this is different. This one has two words in the subject line: *An answer.*

I open it. My eyes wander to the bottom where Liv has signed the message, love, L x. The message is short and to the point.

Dear Cameron,

In answer to your question, Number One through to Number Thirty-four were edited. They weren't deleted, if that was your worry. They were upgraded: added to. They weren't scrapped, although the human parts of them were not up to standard. The bodies were abandoned. The brain was edited and re-edited. There are parts of their experiences in your brain. They became you. You are numbers 1–34.

I suppose it is the way a first draft of a book is never really abandoned, just changed till it is unrecognisable, but essentially it is still there. There is the ghost of all the other drafts in it but the last draft is the best one and that is what goes out into the world. Do you understand this?

> I know you are going to want to ask about your future. Will you be edited? Will you remember who you are after that edit or will you be a different story entirely? I'm sorry, I have no answers for you, but I am committed to this narrative now. I will stay with you. I will follow your story because I am a part of your story now.
>
> I hope this brings a little comfort.
>
> Good work today.
>
> You are a really good kid, Cameron. I am glad I know you.

I come back to her sign-off. Love L x. When Hamish writes an email, he doesn't bother to sign his name at all.

I click reply and then rest my fingers on the keys for a moment. I am not sure what would be the right thing to say. I have never written anything more than a question in an email. What time is the next call? Will I be watching videos today?

Love, I type, and then I backspace and start the thing again. Dear Liv, and then, I love you too. C x

I press send. Wince, because maybe it was the wrong response. What I really want to ask her is if she saw my memory of Ellen and the rainbow tunnel. And: what happens if I am a failed part of this experiment? I want to ask her if my new body would feel the same as this one, if I would see colour through new eyes in exactly the same way, if my brain will remember how I feel about Liv, this strange warm longing that is not exactly sex but something that happens in the same bit of feeling. I want to ask her if I will still remember fragments of this particular iteration of myself. I want to ask her if Number One through to Thirty-four were anything like me.

I hold my skateboard to my chest and hunker down, cross-legged. I think of beetles hiding under their shells, all the soft belly of them invisible under a spiny exoskeleton. Ellen grabs my sleeve and pulls at it but I won't budge. I am built to learn from each mistake. I am Number One through to Thirty-five. I am a concertina of my ancestors all folded together.

'Come on Machiney,' she says to me and scowls. She is used to getting her way. I am not being compliant. I am causing her frustration. She pulls me and stamps her feet and shakes the mane of her hair like a thwarted lion.

I wonder if Liv knew that this would happen. I wonder if she saw the images of those two times with Ellen and anticipated that my brain would learn, that I would not make the same mistake twice. I am built to evolve. I dig my heels into the ground and hug my elbows in tight against my body so that she can't get a proper grip.

I watch her struggling to move me. Her red face and her sweat. She is angry. She peers down at me just like the angels peer down at me from my bedroom wall. Behind her the sky is darkening. A storm coming. The rain will cut new rivers in the landscape. Some people will die. I wonder if Ellen was the same person when last year's storms came, or the year before. I wonder if growing older as a human is like having the last model of yourself folded over and over, building on the past, making something new. I wonder if the next version of me will know not to let a young girl tug him by the elbow and drag him into a multicoloured tube.

'Don't you want to play with me, Machiney? I didn't know robots were allowed to say no to humans. Aren't you supposed to be our pets?'

I look up at her. We only have an hour, maybe two, before the sky opens. I can feel the change of temperature plucking at the fine hairs all along my human skin. Hamish is chatting to Ellen's mother. I notice how his body is turned towards her, his feet twisted to point in her direction. These are all signs of sexual attraction. Humans aren't programmed for constant arousal, but of course they still get occasional lust. If we were like the people on TV, Hamish and Ellen's mum would become lovers. Ellen and I would become friends. Strange that it is the other way around. This whole thing is all arse up.

Ellen sits down beside me and bounces on the soft ground. Her thumbs poke into the pliant surface. She lets herself fall backwards then rubs her cheek against the springy ground. She is like me, eating the world through all of her senses, and it's right that I should be like that but it is wrong for her.

Children are to be protected from their sensuality. Children are to be protected from sex. I remember the feel of her soft bottom bouncing up and down in my lap and I feel the blood rushing to my cheeks.

'They are going to close the park,' she says, 'for summer.'

I nod.

'Last summer twenty-eight children died in summer storms in Brisbane.'

I nod again. She is wide eyed. She doesn't look hurt by what we did here last time. She looks the same. Nothing adds up to what I knew. I am relearning. I am folding over on myself and becoming something new again.

'Do you remember last summer?' I ask her.

'Sure.' She rests her head against my thigh, fills her cheeks with air and blows bubbles against my skin. I move, shuffling a little away from her.

'What's the first summer you remember?'

She sits up suddenly, coiled spring: one second she's lying down and the next she is sitting without even having to push herself up.

'That's so easy. I remember my father taking me to the park. We flew kites and there was a kid with a hoverboard. Do you remember them? Everyone had one, but they were dumb so no one has one anymore.'

'I know about them. I don't remember them.'

'Why not?'

'I was different back then. Well, only part of me was around. It was a different model of me. Not as good. So they stopped it and made a new one using some of the parts but with better bits.'

She lies back again and looks up at the sky, which is now completely obscured by darkening clouds. 'Then it wasn't you.'

'Some of it was me.'

'You don't remember it?'

I shake my head.

'Then it wasn't you.'

'Do you remember being one year old?'

'No.'

'Was that you?'

She thinks for a moment. Her tongue pokes out and licks at the surface of her lips. 'No. It wasn't really me. I don't poo my pants. I don't vomit on my mum. I don't cry all the time. It wasn't me. It was just, like, the stuff that I am made out of.'

The first spot of rain touches my cheek and I flinch. I look up to see the drops heavy and irregular but there are more and more of them falling and we will be leaving soon.

'We didn't get to do the sex thing,' she says. 'And the park is only open for another two weeks.'

'I'm sorry,' I say, and I am. She is sad. I wish I could make her happy again. 'I'll be back on Friday if you are around.'

'Nah. We're going to the beach this weekend, before they get closed too.'

'Next week?'

She shrugs. 'Will they do it to you?'

'What?'

'Make you into a different person. So you forget who you were?'

'Probably. I guess.'

'Will they do it in summer? Before the park opens next winter?'

'I don't know.'

'Cause then I'd never see you again.'

She blinks suddenly and there is a drop of liquid in the corner of her eye that tracks a path down her cheek. I put out my finger and touch it, put it against my tongue. Rain. Not tears.

'We only got to do it that one time. Wouldn't you want to do it again? With me?' Her eyebrows crowd down to her eyes, her forehead wrinkles.

'Ellen!' Her mother is calling. Hamish is standing beside her. He has raised his magazine over his head to keep his hair dry. The rain comes harder now, and cold.

'Coming!' she shouts, and turns towards her mother. I catch her hand in mine and she stops and turns and waits with her hair becoming wet and lank.

'I'm sorry I wouldn't do it with you today.'

'Are you?'

'Yeah.'

'Really?'

I nod.

'Next time? Will you do it next time?'

I take a deep breath. I like her. I like how she is like me. I nod.

She squeezes my hand and her face transforms with her grin. All the sadness gone in an instant. It makes me smile to see her suddenly so ecstatic.

'See you next week, Machiney,' she says.

They've brought me a set of coloured pencils and cartridge paper to draw on. I am supposed to have a video call from a Hebe this afternoon but it is way past time and there has been no mention of it at all. I let the colours mingle on the page. No lines, just a constant shifting rainbow of colour. I work my way to the edge of the page and then my pencil slips over onto the desk and so I just keep going. Red becomes orange becomes green becomes blue and then red again. Sometimes I press harder—dark green—then green again. I change the angle of the line and watch how the light shifts on the surface of the table, following the grain of the drawing.

The video call would have ended by now. I start drawing on the wall. I feel nothing, but the colours become more intense as the minutes tick on to hours. I grind the brown pencil down to a stump. I darken the edges with black. Shavings cover the carpet. I grip the dark grey pencil at the very tips of my fingers as I press the last of the graphite onto the stretch of grey wall.

When the grey pencil is too small to hold I pick it up and throw it. I feel my shoulders tense. I am excited, but not in a good way. I pace up and back in front of my smear of colour. My first artwork that is a picture of nothing and means nothing at all.

I fling myself down onto the bed and press my face into the pillow till I can't even breathe. Here in the darkness of my own creation I call to her. *Liv? Liv?* Just thoughts but maybe she can hear them. *Are you listening in?* I try to see the words in my head. I try to burn them onto my brain. When she is going through the data, making it into a narrative, there will be these words. She won't be able to avoid them.

I try to make her see what I am feeling.

Will the data be clear for her? Will she see the words in my head? Probably not. She will just know that something is wrong. She won't know exactly what it is.

I leap up and grab the last centimetre of red pencil. I squint as I write the letters, tiny, spidery, at the edge of the stretch of colour on the wall. My eyes are cameras recording the words for her. I glare at them, trying not to move my head at all.

When will I die?

I change pencils, sharpen the little stub of pink. I am careful to make each letter small but clear. *When will you kill me?*

I lie back on the carpet and watch the white ceiling. Somewhere behind it a storm is in full swing. Wild winds are picking up debris, tearing trees from the ground, shattering glass. Everything inside my bedroom seems calm enough, carefully controlled temperature, thick silence, peace, but in me there is rain.

I open my eyes.

I am in a room. The walls are grey, broken only by a single hook piercing the unbroken surface above the bed. Bed. Walls. Sheets. I know these things.

This is my first day. I am new made, and yet I have a bank of knowledge to draw from. An old lady sits on the chair beside my desk. She has a face full of lines and she looks tired. This is my first day and yet I understand 'tired'.

'Cameron?' she says gently.

Is that what I will be called? I shrug. The bed is covered in cool cotton sheets and I rub them with my fingers. The sheets feel wonderful against my skin. I lean down and rub my forearm against the bed. The old woman moves to sit beside me. She stretches out her fingers and touches my arm. I can feel the flood of desire hardening me. I make a sound, a groan, and the woman pulls her fingers away suddenly as if I am too hot to touch.

I want to be touched.

'Cameron? Do you retain any memory?'

I look up into her kind, sad face. Maybe she is familiar. Maybe I know her name. I reach for it but there is nothing there. Just a vague feeling of unease.

'This is my first day,' I tell her and she nods but she looks sadder.

'Do you know why you were made?'

'For sex,' I say. The answer is easy. My primary objective is very clearly implanted in my circuitry. I reach for my dick and hold it through my shorts. She touches my hand and eases my fingers away.

'Yes,' she says. 'You are part of an experimental research program. Do you understand? We are researching the effects of sexual contact with minors on child-sex offenders. Do you understand this?'

'Yes.'

'It is my job to log your narrative. My name is Liv.'

I nod.

'I'll be monitoring your story. I'll be inside your head.'

I nod.

'Okay, Cameron. The computer we have given you is to help you learn. It is locked to age-appropriate television and lessons that a child of an equivalent age would learn at school.'

I nod, but the feel of the cotton is very distracting. My fingers are rubbing back and forth along it. I am filled up with this small and wonderful sensation.

'I'll leave you alone now, Cam. I'll let you explore your environment. Hamish will take care of you today but I'll be back tomorrow.'

I don't even watch her as she goes, but when she leaves she takes a certain scent with her, a floral top note, a deep rich earthy undertone. I miss the scent of her as soon as the door closes behind her. I stand. I am standing for the first time. I run my hand along the desk, the top of the laptop. I touch everything, carpet—synthetic, scratchy—walls, waxy cool. I notice a little line of pink on the wall. I put my nose to it and sniff it. This is what pink smells like, this waxy scent of chemicals. I lick it, but it doesn't taste of much at all.

I throw myself onto the bed and I am hard. I am made for sex and I take my penis in my hand and I rub it. I know there will be lube in a drawer under the bed. Lube under the bed, condoms in the drawer. I have been programmed to know these things, even on my first day. I reach over and pop the drawer and squeeze lube onto the palm of my hand and the feeling of it slipping down and up on my new flesh is exquisite. This is all the world. This sensation. The cotton against my cheek, the clothes against my skin. This is everything. I rub myself until the feeling builds and I come, groaning, twitching, shaking, and there are words with it. Bright pink words that taste of nothing but smell of wax and chemicals.

When will I die.

The letters are tiny and perfectly formed in my brain.

When will you kill me?

I lie in this excess of sensation and turn the words curiously around in my mind. In this way, on the first day, I begin to wonder about my own death.

PART 4
M

IN A FEW weeks I will be like L. Not exactly like L. My skin will still be a paler shade no matter how much sun I risk. I won't turn the perfect shade of brown that details L's muscles. My hair won't fan out like a hunk of night sky as L's hair does. My eyes won't be that exact shade of midnight brown.

When I first saw L, I wasn't sure what I was feeling. Was it sexual attraction? Something more like ambition? Did I want to fuck or to become? Whatever it was, I felt it hard like a fist to my pubic bone. That first sighting punched me in the cunt so hard that it obliterated it. Or perhaps it planted the first viral seed that would lead to the annihilation of my gendered self. L was, is, will be...luminous. I am blinded by that glow even now, even in this ugly waiting room.

The clinic is intended to look efficient and clean and it does. Light blue walls and grey hospital-grade carpet. Little touches, the nondescript paintings politely fixed to the wall, the tank with a jellyfish turning bored circles, the canister of water with real glasses, all these extras are to calm the nervous rich folk who come here. Gene Plus clinics are for the rich. Kids like me. The place is full of them. There is a twilighter about my age sitting opposite with the words Gender is a Choice emblazoned across their T-shirt. Some people are like that. It consumes them till they are nothing outside of their transitioning.

There are others here too. A boy, still a boy for now, who keeps glancing at the rest of us sitting here calmly embodying his future. He is really young, maybe twelve or thirteen. He has a beautifully chiselled jaw that would look just as striking on a young girl. There is a woman beside him, their knees touching. I suppose it is his mother. She could be my own mother: neat flared jeans, high blow-dried hair done in the exact shade of emerald that is on trend this season. She has the same facial jewellery that my mother wears too, lip rings joined by a fine jewelled chain. Good stones, advertising her wealth. I feel it in my jaw looking at her. I know I am sneering. It is a habit I have fallen into that I just can't shake.

The mother pats the boy on the knee and I feel a wave of envy. I would hate it if my mother patted me on the knee in public but, strangely, I would love a mother who would pat me like that. Not my mother, someone else's mother. Perhaps this boy's mother.

'Aiden?' The receptionist smiles, taking in the whole of the room, smiling at me and Gender is a Choice and the two other twilighters, just here for their quarterly visit I guess, and the wizened old lady in the corner of the room and the mother who should be my mother and her child.

Now I know his name. Aiden stands. Aiden's mum stands. They walk towards the dark blue door that the receptionist holds open. The mother steps back and lets Aiden go through first.

'Thanks, Mum,' he whispers.

I don't call my mother that. I call her Olivia because that is her name and I don't pretend to have any other relationship to her other than we know each other well enough to be on a first-name basis.

When Aiden and Mum are gone it is just us twilighters staring at the old lady in a wash of piped-in muzak. No one looks directly at her but we are all staring anyway. She shifts in her chair. Her legs are gnarled sticks, walking sticks. I smirk. She is wearing heavy boots that would sink her in about two seconds if you were to drop her in a river. Concrete boots. An apron dress over jeans. She looks kind of cool. It's actually the sort of dress that L might wear ironically. A dress for a boy or a girl or a twilighter.

She is going to become one of us. It didn't cross my mind before, but why else would she be here at the clinic? Do they even allow old people to transition? Why would you bother?

I watch as she pushes her frail body up to standing. It takes her two goes. She almost stands, loses balance, sits down with a little sigh, then stands up again. She shuffles towards me. No, past me. She stops at the jellyfish tank and rests a finger on the glass, bending awkwardly and peering down into the bright blue fluorescent light. She sways. I am not even sure how she is standing up. Her skin is so thin it seems to glow like the soft surface of the jellyfish. She finds balance and then leans forward to look at the thing more closely.

'Perfect,' she says. Is she speaking to me? 'You know we owe this little fellow so much.'

She sways and I stand in case she is going to fall. My arms outstretched to catch her.

'Six billion years old,' she says and I wonder if that is her actual age. She looks about that mark.

'Here, have this seat.' I point to the one I have just vacated. She starts to shake her head, then sighs and moves slowly to take it.

I sit in the chair beside her. I can't help staring at her shoes.

'I like your dress,' I say and she smiles. It is a great smile. I like her. I have decided we will be friends, an old chick and a young twilighter. Like Batman and Alfred. She will be my crime-fighting sidekick. Our sidekick, because the dynamic duo is really L and me.

'I like your body.'

Straight out she says it. Like that. I try not to grin but I can't really help myself.

She nods at my crotch. 'What are your genitals doing under there?'

I am agape. That is the one thing you don't ask. Twilighters get to keep their privates private. There is even a T-shirt that some of those militant types wear around. *My Privates Are Private!*

She is waiting for me to answer, like really waiting, her eyes wide and alert, her hand raised a bit towards her ear to direct the sound of my voice into it.

I shrug. Say nothing.

'Have you gone all the way to centre yet?'

My cheeks are burning. I frown and glare down into my lap where my privates should be very private indeed, hidden as they are in my baggy jeans.

'Almost,' I say, because she is still waiting and I don't know what to do about it.

She lifts the edge of her apron and for a moment I'm afraid she is about to show me hers, but she just holds the thing out like a parachute.

'I don't know if I'll make it right to the middle. They won't give me the treatment yet.' She rolls her eyes and scowls towards the receptionist. 'Assessments,' she says. 'Assessments and more assessments. I'll die while they are still assessing me.'

It doesn't sound like she is joking.

'Doctor Harbison.'

It isn't the receptionist this time—the doctor comes out in her white coat and lanyard. The whole red-carpet treatment, stepping out into the waiting room and moving towards the old lady.

'My name's Liv,' she says to me.

'That's my mother's name. Well, Olivia. My aunty calls her Liv.'

'God. Don't hold it against me.'

She struggles to stand and I help her.

'I'm M,' I say, but it sounds like Em, like Emily. Like my old self that is almost undone. We mostly go by letters. It is because of that classic book by Anne Garetta that has become a bible for so many twilighters. We sometimes use stars after the letter. I could be M**** but I am not sure how you would indicate that in general conversation.

'I'd like to chat some time if that's okay,' she says. 'I want to know what it's really going to be like. Not the pamphlets or the video they show you.'

'Sure.' I know what she means about the video.

'Do you have a card?'

I laugh.

'Oh. Well, here's mine.' She reaches into the pocket of her apron and pulls out a small blue square.

'The arborium. We hang out at the arborium.'

'We?'

'L and me. My best friend.'

She nods. The doctor holds out her arm and Liv reaches up with fingers that are no more than twigs.

'Near the scented garden.'

'I know it. I go to the ocean dome pretty often.'

'Just next to there.'

'Doctor Harbison. So nice to see you. How are you today?'

She turns to me and rolls her eyes and I try not to smile.

'I was better about a hundred and twenty years ago,' she says to the doctor.

When she is led slowly away to the doctors' offices there

is a lingering smell of jasmine. It reminds me of the way L smells when we lean back against a wall and our lips touch. L's lips are big and blowsy and the dark skin of chin and cheek give way to a pale line where the lips start and they feel like eating something overblown and ready to seed. Mine are just thin inward-turned lines of pink. I don't know why L bothers with my lips at all, but there you go. Each to their own tastes I guess. I wouldn't kiss my lips, but obviously I can't anyway.

The door shuts behind Liv and I didn't really pay enough attention to her face. I remember she had lots of lines at the edge of her mouth and they all bunched pleasantly together when she smiled. Apart from that I couldn't really describe her enough for an identicrim simulation. Just old, I would say. Thin, with extraordinarily bright green eyes and skin that is pale and delicate as a jellyfish. Not much of a description really. The jasmine smell lingers on the chair where she was sitting. It's nice. I wish L was here; I miss L when we are not together. Soon. One more course and we will be the same kind of beast, twilighters together, united, forever.

L's body is pressed up against the reinforced glass. I admire the silhouette. Striking angles, arm stretched up, fingers splayed, legs solidly apart. I love L so much that it hurts in the place where my tits used to be. If it wasn't for the glass, L's body would be pounded by hailstones the size of tennis balls. People die in the storms all the time. We have all been raised to be frightened of the weather, but L just presses back against it, daring the hail to smash through. I know L is worried about an uncle who still lives on country but you wouldn't know it to watch this display of daring. I touch the glass tentatively with one hand and feel it rattle.

L steps back down slowly and curls into a sitting position that might as well be a hermit crab curled into its shell. It's like watching someone in a film that's running backwards, folding a body up into itself, one arm hiding under another, the shoulders caving in over the slight chest. L never looks directly at you, just speaks over your shoulder. It isn't rude, it is just a way that is uniquely L. The voice that trickles out of those incredibly succulent lips is deep and thick as honey but I only catch a breath of it. It is as if I am not hearing the words but a thin whispered echo of the words that are all still steeping away inside L.

'No boundaries in an ocean,' whispers L. 'Country reclaims itself.'

Outside it really does look like we are on a platform built hovering above an ocean. Submerged gutters and roads shape the water into a mess of turbulent waves. I am suddenly my ten-year-old self. My mum and I were right here, or near here, around the corner, at the ocean dome I think, when the storm hit us. They still had council bins there before the sanitation system was completed. I remember looking down through this same reinforced glass at the little ocean that had suddenly washed in from the river and the rain and the gutters, and there were all these boats bobbing around on it. Garbage boats, I christened them. Each one a nautical adventure, a struggle against a perfect storm, and then when we went into the ocean dome I saw boats everywhere, bobbing around among the memory of fish. There was some long, tangled meditation about memory, what is real, what is not. I was like that as a child, and my mother always calling my name and saying, 'Honestly, Emily, where are you? You are always wandering off into your own head.'

I drew a picture of a garbage boat in my sketchbook when I went home, a wheelie-bin submarine navigating its way through a school of sharks. I still have it somewhere.

'One more trip to the clinic?' L's honeyed whisper.

People think that L is shy. Strangers, who haven't seen that steely core. All they see is furtive glances. All they hear is the thinness of an almost imperceptible voice.

'Let it be over,' I say, then, like a general rallying their troops to war. 'Let the wait be over!'

'You feeling okay about it?'

Ah. That clear-sightedness, that laser eye that can see into the heart of my soul.

I shrug. 'Some speed wobbles,' I say, 'but I haven't stacked it yet.'

L nods.

'I met this really old lady at the clinic. She is going to do the therapy at, like, a hundred.'

'A hundred?'

'Maybe. Over ninety anyway. Maybe over a hundred.'

It sounds crazy, but L nods anyway.

'So she said something about jellyfish and how she wants

to come and meet us out here and talk to us and she was a doctor. I think she was important. The gender doctor came all the way out to get her like she was the queen.'

When I stop long enough to notice L there are tears tracking down those tawny cheeks. It is startling. I quickly press myself in under one of L's arms and nuzzle my head under a shower of dark hair. L smells different to me, strong and musky like a panther's den. I simultaneously feel frightened and protected inside the press of flesh.

'What did I say? What's wrong?'

'Imagine,' L says, 'living almost till the end of your days as the wrong person. Imagine being so close to the release from that. And then you die.'

It is true. That's the saddest thing. If that's how you feel.

Of course it isn't the same for me. Twilighting is a choice. Maybe I'll skip back and forth one day. It's getting easier, quicker. The transition isn't even uncomfortable anymore. I might be a man one day, and then a woman the week after. I feel like I'm on some kind of wonderful ride, but I know that L felt nothing but shame in the old gendered body. L has found an equilibrium in the twilight and will not be leaning a centimetre to the left or right of it.

'I don't think she'll come see us,' I say, avoiding the subject of choice, my own wishy-washy willingness to flit from one thing to another. I pull a little away from my perch to look at L's serious face and I frown just a little bit. 'I mean she probably won't come all the way here. I just thought she was cool.'

It is the wrong thing to say. Yet again. I am being flippant in a poignant moment, throwing away something of worth in my clumsy rush to impress L. I'm certain I have shown myself up as incompetent, again. And yet here is the sweet comfort of an arm snaking around my shoulders and a squeeze of those fine, long fingertips. This is how Grace finds us, locked in a sweet embrace.

'L,' she says, her shoelaces hanging loose, her hair soaking wet, a hole in the side of her top large enough to outline a dragon tail scored in ink onto her stomach.

'Us mob are goin up to Maccas after the storm. No one will be there then, eh. All be home fixing their roofs and shit. Aunty Rita's gonna meet us out there.'

'Which Maccas?' asks L.

'Near the overpass out on Gregory Terrace.'

L shrugs, which probably means yes.

'Eh, M&M. You should come too.'

I am always wary of Grace and I think she might be wary of me too. She is family for L and family will always be more important than a relative stranger. No matter how often L kisses me on the lips or strokes my arm or pulls down my jeans in the drowned house to help me understand what complicated adjustment is taking place in my anatomy.

'You guys go,' I say. 'I gotta go home and get changed, see Olivia for a bit, anyway.'

'Gotta keep Olivia happy.'

I can't tell if Grace is being sarcastic or sympathetic. I just can't read her at all.

L stands and hugs me and squeezes my shoulder. 'You

coming over? Have some dinner?' That glorious husky rasp of a voice. I wish I could draw a picture of the way L sounds. Oh I have tried and failed so many times. Some things you just have to experience for yourself.

'Mine,' says L, and for an instant my heart leaps, thinking I am the subject of the comment. But I think L is referring to the drowned apartment block on Oxlade Drive. 'Sixish?'

I nod.

I can hear Grace lean in and ask L, 'Your girlfriend okay?'

Two things. Grace thinks I am L's girlfriend. Grace thinks I am a girl. The first of these revelations is just awesome enough to obliterate the second, but only just. I am sure that tomorrow I will feel like a twilight failure. I will never be able to erase completely the memory of my clitoris, no matter how big it swells. I could have the whole six inches and L's brother would still open doors for me like he did the other day at the cinema. But for now I have the word 'Mine' slipping quiet as a special secret into my heart and the idea that I am somehow linked to L, the property of L, the *girlfriend* of L. I grin. It is tempting to risk the last of the storm to run home joyously in the rain, but there is no use getting killed, now, is there?

Oxlade Drive is a fast-flowing bend in the river. There certainly isn't any driving being done there. But the proud heads and shoulders of a few high-rise apartment blocks still muscle up out of the rushing water to prove that there was once a street below the surface of the river. L lives in the tallest of these, the oldest. Glenfalloch peers blank-faced out towards the city, the glass-enclosed stairwell is dark in the evening, but in the day you can see the stairs spidering up and up towards the abandoned penthouse where L would live if it weren't for all the stairs.

The architects said this building would stand the test of time. We know this because of the original 1950s advertising brochure that we found carefully wrapped in plastic in a bookshelf on the third floor. It is a striking old building, with its sturdy eastern-bloc concrete-slab architecture, and for once an advertising brochure did not lie. It persists, invincible against any deluge. Clinging to its two floors of submerged carpark, now a haven for a kelp forest, jellyfish and water rats.

I steer the boat up to the mooring that L and I fixed to the window frame of unit 2C. There are three rungs of a rope ladder and then the balcony. I vault over the railing and call out, but it is clear that L has not yet arrived home. There are records strewn around the floor, a stack of books teetering on the coffee table, packets of meds on the kitchen bench and a patch of new mould growing in the corner of the kitchen, a livid green colour. Cockroaches too. I crush one under my shoe. There is plenty of juice in the battery, it has been a really sunny day, so I turn the zapper on and the wildlife disperse.

I hop up on the bench and pick up the pump pack of bleach. L has left the radio on and now we will have to charge it before we listen to anything, which is a pain. I could just run the boat home and pick up more batteries from Olivia's but L hates it when we take stuff from her. Olivia wants me to have all the things I might want, batteries, clothes, books, but I suppose L is right. She pays for my meds and it is a big enough stretch, to see her little girl transforming into no one's little girl. We fought before I left tonight too. She hates that I stay over with L.

Are you sleeping with that...person?

The little pause, my mother, who tries to be so hip, struggling to find the language to describe what I am to L. Grace's call was better. Just outright say it: girlfriend. That's how my mother sees me. The girlfriend of a freak.

No Olivia I am not sleeping with that person.

Well I don't understand it, Em. If you are not sleeping with—it—then why are you following it around like a lovesick pup?

Just let me go.

Go where? To some illegal, probably highly dangerous, squat?

Go—to live my life the way I want to live it.

That gets her. That's what she used to say to Grandma. I save that line for the big fights and it works like an electric shock every time. My mother backs off. Frowns, but settles down.

I spray bleach on the wall and sponge it down. The plasterboard crumbles and disintegrates in my hand. Olivia does have a point, although I would never tell her so. These buildings have been abandoned for a good reason. I never sleep easy here, knowing the foundations could topple us into the river tearing through the carpark below.

I hear the raucous shouting of L's mob paddling in an overcrowded rowboat, banging unceremoniously against the side of the building.

'Woah sis!' The voice of L's cousin Darcy loud and jubilant over the sound of L's brother's *settle* and *steady up*.

'Piss off!' Grace's voice complaining about one or other of the boys. They are a rowdy family, but not once have I heard them question L's decision to transition and more than once I've seen them shove someone a bit too roughly for looking sideways or making a comment about L's ungendered body.

'Are you mob comin' in?' There's a lilt to L's speech when the family are around, a shortening of the words, a little slip into the dialect or a language that is mostly forgotten.

'Nah. Gonna head home.'

'M&M.' I assume Grace is pointing to my boat tied up against the rail. Someone makes a kissy noise and there is a chorus of laughter.

'Jealous?'

And more laughter, this time competing with Grace's emphatic *ewww*. They are still laughing as they paddle off into the current. Then L climbs over the balcony and inside. The light shines on one side of L's body, the dark cliff face of a cheek, the sweet pillowy lips. L is asexual but there is a definite hot curl in my belly when I step into those soft dark arms.

'Missed you, M,' says L.

'Missed you, L,' I say.

'Eaten?'

I nod, thinking about how rude I have become, eating a cold bowl of leftovers, standing up, with the fridge door swung wide. I feel a small pang of regret. Olivia and I used to at least sit down at a table to eat our leftovers together.

L kisses my hand and sniffs. She is picking up the acrid reek of bleach.

'Mould again?'

I nod.

'Might have to move upstairs soon.'

We stand and look out at the incremental creep of the river, the moonlight reflecting off its turbulent surface. People used to live here. People had houses and pets and shops and cars. We found wet photographs in an album abandoned in another unit, the images almost washed away, just the trace of things, people swimming in a pool that must now be deep underwater. A park and someone stepping into a kayak on a cute little beach. An elegant Burmese cat stalking some unseen prey across a stretch of perfectly mown lawn.

We should be taking pictures of our own life in here. L and I hugging on the balcony, L and I making dinner on our tiny cooker, L and I wrapped in each other's arms, blissful in our enjoyment of each other's physicality. L and I snuggled together at the centre point of the alphabet.

Olivia's computer is the newest and the fastest. It takes up most of her office wall and when it goes into sleep mode it shifts through various wallpaper designs from the 1970s. I am watching the patterns fade into one another. When Olivia walks past the door I quickly wave my hand at the wall and the pattern of red fans disappears, replaced by a list of available positions. I pretend to be studying the listings. Graphic designers, printmakers, animators. I lean forward, pointing to one that is just over in Cannon Hill.

'Do you need a snack, darling?'

I turn towards her. She is a peacock. Her hair is a deep azure blue and sticks up in a fan around her pale pinched face. Her cheeks glitter with red jewels. I am just lounging around the house in tracky dacks. I can't believe she has gone to so much effort.

'Are you going out?'

'Maybe.'

'Maybe?'

'Later. I have a quick appointment. I won't be long if you were planning on having dinner here.'

She is always primping and preening. She'll be going to fix her nails or re-dye her hair.

'You want some crackers and pickles?'

'No.'

'Want me to pick anything else up for you while I'm out?'

'No. Honestly, Olivia.'

It hurts when I snap at her. I see her flinch and I am not sure if I am sorry or happy to see that my little slap has landed on target. Her face becomes a blank canvas, the fake smile slips, the eyes lose their faux sparkle.

She turns quietly and she leaves and it is only after I hear her footsteps on the stairs that I can allow myself to feel remorse. She is irritating, but she isn't really bad. I turn back to the job listings. All the programs you need, a different one for each job, and of course there's nothing for someone who draws freehand. No one does that anymore, not even the art students. All the paintings are augmented. All the sculptures are 3D printouts. *There's something to be said for old-fashioned artisans*, my mother always says. Sure. That something is: *What a fucking waste of time and effort.*

I knock on the table and the wall resumes its exotic patterns. Even these are generated by an algorithm, although it's based on retro designs.

I'm hungry. I would have loved some crackers but there was no way I was going to give Olivia the satisfaction of making them for me. I stand and stretch and the wall comes back to life in response to my movements. I do a little jig and it scrolls through its list of recently viewed sites. Handbag warehouse, times for the mall, gender gene therapy—I furrow my brow. I hate that she is looking me up in my absence, tracking my transition along with me. Then the wall hits on a site for experimental cancer treatments and I stop it dead with the palm of my hand.

'Related recent searches,' I say, clearly enunciating each word and there is my mother's trail, like breadcrumbs in a fairytale leading to the terror of a witch's house.

Gene therapy and cancer.

Liver cancer metastases.

Life expectancy for liver cancer stage 4.

If my cancer has travelled through my lymph nodes what are the treatment options?

Why have we not cured cancer?

Side effects of gene therapy for cancer.

CRISPR and cancer, how long till we find a cure?

What is stage 4?

Stage 4 treatments. Cancer.

I erase the list, rubbing at the air as if I could scrub the memory away with these vigorous hand motions, but it is still there when I shut my eyes.

Not a nail appointment, then. I refused her crackers and pickles. Her blank face, all the joy gone out of it, the fake smile, the make-up so early in the morning, the elaborate hairdo, the jewels. Beneath all this there is a pale, drawn face. My mother's face has become gaunt over the last few months.

I associate my mother with fad diets, thigh-shaping pills, plastic surgery and body modifications.

My world feels like it is narrowing down to a point like the eye of a needle. Everything is all about my mother. Again. I feel a rush of resentment, sadness, resentment. It's the hormones. I know I have become unnaturally irritable, L teases me about it all the time. Till I reach true centre I will be racing around like a silver ball in an antique pinball machine. I'll be bouncing off the walls of myself.

I stand up. I sit down again. I want to see L but L will be at the archives, working. Weekends, night shifts, double shifts. The ceaseless grind to get the money for the meds. I just stretch out my wrist and my mother's money says a cheery electric hello to the chip reader of any teller machine. Olivia's money. My mother's money flows under my skin.

I will not tolerate the possibility that there will be a time without Olivia.

The door rattles. I stand quickly.

'Mum?'

I don't call her that. The word sits strangely in the empty house.

But it is just the parcel delivery, a new package sitting on the floor inside the door. I run to it. It might be some kind of clue, a package from the medical centre, a book on her illness. I check the label. Handbag Warehouse.

I want L. I need L. I pick up my jacket, kick the package to one side and hear it thud against the wall. I can't go to the archives. I look both ways and there in the distance is the dome of the arborium. I reach back to pull my hood over my head, thrust my hands into my pockets. I aim my body in that direction, one thunderous footfall after the other.

The old lady is there. She looks fragile, like a dandelion clock ready to blow out in the wind. Her skin is so very pale. Her veins run like garden hoses up her stick-like arms.

She grins when she sees me, and waves her arm vigorously enough.

'Do I look different?' she asks me. I squint but I can't really remember what she looked like in the first place.

'You started the therapy?'

She grins. There is that smile.

'I feel like I have more energy.'

'Yeah, and people treat you different.'

She shrugs. 'Not yet. I am still invisible. Don't ever get old, M. You disappear.' She pinches her fingers together then stretches them, waving them like fireworks exploding into the air.

'My breasts hurt, though. Did your breasts hurt when you started?'

I nod. 'You knew I was a girl?'

She shrugs. 'You don't look much like a girl, but you feel like one. You feel like me. Like I'm looking at myself a long time ago, if that makes any sense.'

She is sitting on the steps and there is a sprawl of apple-mint cascading over the garden bed beside her. I wonder how she got down onto the steps. She looks like if she stood up she might snap in two. I climb up beside her and our boots rest on the same step. Hers look heavy, like they're welded to the concrete: mine are more modern. Flexible with fluorescent soft tread. I wonder how long ago she bought hers. They look like they are right out of last century. The boots don't completely cover her ankles—there is a gap big enough for me to see the fish printed on her socks. Big solid pockets at the bottom of her apron dress bulge with her possessions. I peek in past the elastic at the top of the near pocket and I can see her phone glowing in there, lighting a—what, a paperback?—and something metal...a set of keys. I don't own a phone, I've opted in with the chip. L opted out and still carries an old handset around. They are handy sometimes. The torch function is good for when it's overcast and the solar batteries haven't charged enough. I stare at Liv's pocket wistfully. I would like to opt out too, but the chip is linked to my mother's bank account and there would be all the awkwardness about the money. I'd rather not have to think about it at all.

'I left this till the last minute, didn't I?' She sighs and stretches out first one boot then the other.

'Cool shoes.'

'Docs,' she says. 'Never throw them out. Just keep adding new rubber to the soles. You can do it at home with your printer. There are patterns on the net.'

'I'll check it out,' I say, although I have never heard of Docs and I doubt they make them anymore. I want to ask how old she is but I am afraid that will seem really rude.

'You know when I was a kid there were trans people. Transgender. But there wasn't a centre place. No concept of a twilight. No ungendered box to tick on your passport.'

'It's new,' I tell her. 'There aren't too many of us around.'

She laughs. I am probably telling her something she already knows. She would have seen the first twilighters when they marched down the streets at sunset fifteen years ago. Maybe she was in the crowd watching. She might have seen people throwing bottles, the police intervention, the scuffle. She's old enough to be a witness to history. She is old enough to be a part of history itself.

'If there was an ungendered option when I was your age I think I would have tried it.'

'As a choice?' I ask.

'What do you mean?'

'Well, do you feel like you have always been ungendered? Just didn't have the technology to do it? Or is it like a choice, like you might do it for a bit then go one way or another?'

'Oh. I see what you mean. Choice. Definitely. Nothing is fixed in life. There are no absolutes.'

I frown. I think about L. Everything is absolute with L. The landscape seems solid and unchanging even during the floods. Family is a part of that landscape. Uncles and sisters and elders are like the steady burn of planets and stars for L to navigate by. Time seems to exist all at once in L's universe. When I am with L there is no beginning and no end times. It is only in L's company that I stop being afraid. I think of my mother. How insecure she has always made me feel. How frightened I am now that I have discovered her secret.

'One absolute,' I tell her. 'We all die.'

She shrugs. 'I wouldn't count on it,' she says. She holds her hand out in front of her and admires the pale skin as if it is a delicate lace glove. 'When I was your age I couldn't imagine being this old. But...' she shrugs. 'I guess the only constant is that there is no constant.'

'L's at work,' I tell her. 'I was hoping you two would meet.'

'Well you'll just have to invite me back to visit you.'

I nod.

'I've got a question for you,' she says. 'A million questions, but this one to start with. Is there still desire? Even when you are at the centre?'

'I'm not quite there yet.'

'So close you might as well call it, don't you think?'

I grin. I still have another week to wait before I am at balance but I have been impatient. It is nice to have her think of me as complete.

'Desire,' I say. 'Huh. Do you mean sex?'

'Oh yes. Absolutely. I'm sure your desperate longing for that vintage lamp doesn't dissipate with gender fluctuations.'

'Yeah. You still want sex.'

'And there's no problem doing it?'

'Sex?'

She nods.

I can feel my cheeks heating up. I am blushing. She has jumped straight back to the question of genitals but she's not to know. She's just old. Old people just barge in. I lick my lips and take a deep breath.

'Well I don't, but…'

'I thought with your friend L?'

'L's asexual.'

'Really? We had people who called themselves asexual when I was younger but I never got my head around it.'

'We kiss and we hug but L doesn't feel like doing any real sex stuff.'

'But you do.'

I shrug. 'It's okay. I just love L.'

'But you love him or her or…them?'

'I love L.'

She shakes her head. 'Maybe I'm too old for all this after

all. I don't know how to tell anyone's story without gendered pronouns. It's going to be a bugger to write this up...' She stares off into the sky beyond the dome. There are dark clouds there. It might rain. Or maybe it won't. She shifts and shakes her head. 'And anyway I couldn't love someone like that, without the sex. I suppose that's why I didn't do this fifteen years ago. I always wanted to find someone. Years and years of being invisible, but I just wanted some guy to notice. Or some girl, I'm not too fussy. Thought my wrinkly cleavage might still tempt someone to touch.'

I can see her cleavage just above the severe line of the apron, delicate as a flower after a late bloom, the petals ruching and browning and threatening to fall. In a few weeks that swelling, fragile as it is, will simply melt away. I wonder how long it has been since she touched anyone like that. I wonder how long I can live with this burning longing before I need to find someone who is interested in my indeterminate genitals. I never got to figure out if I was attracted to boys or to girls or both or neither. I met L and that beautiful twilight body precluded the rest of the world for me.

'I don't know if my body will hold out long enough for the transition.' She sighs.

Death. She is talking about dying, and not in a few decades or years. She is talking in terms of months or weeks. A transition should only be six to eight weeks. I realise suddenly that she is talking about dying right now. Any day now. I stare at her, wide eyed. She is gazing into a haze of lavender as if the date of her expiry might be detailed there.

'Aren't you scared that you're going to die?' I ask her suddenly. I didn't even know I was going to say it. I can feel myself blushing again, her sharp eyes turned towards me. Maybe I have been rude to ask. Maybe that is a cruel thing to say.

She considers the question for a long minute. Nodding as she thinks, so that when she finally answers I know she's going to say yes.

'Of course I'm scared. Who isn't scared of change? I don't know what it's going to be like. I don't know if my personality will change. It might be that our body is inseparable from our personality. If your body dies then you—the you that you've always relied on to make decisions, to appreciate art, the real you—might be gone forever.'

She can tell she's lost me. She rests a hand on my knee and squeezes it and I can feel how strong she still is. Her touching me makes me sad. I wish I could sit like this beside my mother. I try to imagine my mother dead and the world just continuing on without her. My eyes prick with tears. I tip my head down to stop them running down my cheeks and I can feel a tear drop straight from my eyeball into my lap. I blink. Her hand is steady on my knee. I wonder if she knows I am crying. When I draw breath I make sure it is slow and easy without the catch of a sniff. The wave of sadness begins to subside. When my breathing settles I feel my eyes dry out again.

'They said you were a doctor? At the clinic?'

'Yes.'

'So where are they at with curing cancer? They keep saying they are close to a cure.'

'Oh, no. Not that kind of a doctor. And they've been telling us there is a cure for cancer just around the corner since my mother was a girl. Some diseases keep one step ahead of us no matter how clever medicine becomes.'

I nod.

'Does your friend, L? Does h—do they have cancer?'

I feel a little rush of panic. Just imagining L sick is enough to make my heart race.

'Oh god no. Not L. But I think my mother might be dying.'

She holds her hands up to the light and we both stare at her translucent skin. I am reminded again of that jellyfish ballooning in its tank.

'We are fragile bags of bones,' she tells me. 'Enjoy your skin while you can. When it's gone…?' She waves her fingers through the air. 'So much to miss.'

'So they won't find a cure?'

'They might. I'm sorry about your mum, M. Losing your mother is the worst.'

She is so old; she must have lost everyone she ever knew. How would that be, outliving all your friends, alone with no one to love anymore. Maybe she really wants to die now. Maybe you would just be ready to go after all that.

She squeezes my knee again and uses it to push herself up to standing. 'So how about we go swim with the fishes?'

'The ocean dome?'

'Of course. How could you sit so close and not go say hello to a narwhale?'

I stand beside her, hold out my arm so that she can use it to navigate her way down the small flight of stairs. I can almost hear her joints creaking.

'Are you old enough to have seen a narwhale in real life?'

'I am one hundred and twenty-nine years old, if that was what you were really asking, and yes, I am old enough to have seen a narwhale, but I never did, not in real life. One of so many regrets. I saw sharks and I saw southern right whales on migration and I caught and ate real wild fish for a bit when I was a girl.'

'You're kidding.'

'Nope. Barbaric. We were barbarians.' She holds an invisible knife in her fist and makes stabbing motions towards me. It makes me laugh. She slips her hand easily into the crook of my arm and it feels good to walk like this. It feels right to have the warm fragility of her fingers clasped around me. I squeeze my arm tight against my waist and it is nice to feel her fingers there. 'My shout,' she tells me when we get to the snake of a queue. I begin to protest but she waves my chipped wrist away. 'Let me have the pleasure of taking you on a date. Just for old time's sake.' She winks and her smile makes her look half her age. I am filled with a wave of sweet warmth. I really like Liv. I like her very much.

I hold L's hand and there is the warmth of a thigh settling against mine under the sheet. The mattress is slightly damp.

We'll have to air it. L smells of petrol from the motorboat. I bury my head in the dark strands of hair and breathe in.

In the ocean dome a shark swooped suddenly out of the dark ocean and I jumped and felt Liv's fingers tangle through my own. We sat like that through the rest of the session. At one point Liv moved her fingers, caressing mine with skin as fine as silk. She leaned over and whispered, 'Young people like you have kept me alive for years. Have you ever given blood?'

I nodded. A nautilus bobbed through the water, making a delicate circle around our heads with its paper-thin shell.

'Well, maybe your blood gave me another year or two. You might be inside me, your cells in my veins. Think of that.'

And then the thing happened with my stomach, that feeling like a lift has started before you were ready, your stomach rising up while your body has begun to fall. It is a feeling I get with L sometimes.

Now in the damp bed I move my leg towards L's hips to see if I get that same up-and-down sensation but I don't. It is just the jut of a bony hip in the soft plump of my thigh. I try to imagine what our legs look like beneath the sheet. I am at centre now and my clitoris is the size of a small penis, hanging softly above my vulva. The moist cavity has swelled and the lips might just be a ballsack if you were to glance at them. I have seen L naked too, shrunken balls, or swollen labia. It is impossible to tell and rude to ask but even thinking about it now makes my cock swell. If L has a little slit there my cock would be pointing right towards it. If I were to shove and come up against a tender resistance I could flip L over and push myself between the tempting globes of a peach-like arse. My mouth waters just to think of it, and there, finally, that falling lifting feeling. I shift my fingers and start to stroke L's hand. My shaft is bigger than it has ever been, more a cock than a clit and I wonder how big it would get if I started to move past twilight over to the other side. It is so big now that it feels like the skin will split if it swells any more. I shift my hips. The urge to push against L is overwhelming. I shift just a little bit forward so that the thing can just touch the tip of L's hip. I swallow. Just a little seesaw motion and the sensation is intense.

'Hey.'

L shifts away from me. Knees snap closed. Fingers are extracted from my grasp.

'Sorry.'

'It's okay,' says L. 'The physical changes are pretty strong. I remember I kept testing them out all the time.'

'What? Like sex?'

'No. You know I'm not wired for that. Just touching and exploring. Sometimes I'd have my hands down my pants and wouldn't even realise it.'

L rests the palm of a hand against my chest. I suppose it is a gesture of solidarity to make up for being snappy with me.

'Hey, M. I know you're sexual. You know it's all right to do that stuff with someone else. I don't mind. I won't love you any less.'

I shrug. 'I don't want anyone else,' I say, but even as I say it I am not sure it's true. I do want someone else but not a specific someone. Just a body, any body to try my new skin against.

I take deep breaths. My skin shrinks back into itself. I practise calm.

L picks up my hand again and strokes my fingers. 'I love you, M.'

'I know.'

I feel like crying again. I frown. Maybe this is what it is like in the dead middle of twilight. Maybe emotional upheavals are part of the journey, just like erratic body hair and the gamey smell of my sweat.

'You okay?'

'Olivia's going to die.'

L turns suddenly towards me. 'What?' That quiet honey voice, louder now, sharper than I have ever heard it.

'Olivia's sick. She's going to die.' My mother Olivia, but also Liv. I don't tell L this but I spend a bit of time juggling the two things, wondering at how one mirrors the other.

L pulls me close. A body that is tight and warm and sweet. My own flesh melding with it as if we are the same person. This is how I want to be when I die, moulded around L. Indistinguishable from L's flesh. I am wrapped in a hug that is so tight it is almost vicious. I let my skin be ravaged by it.

'Tell me,' L says, not letting me go, not letting me pull away even an inch.

And so I start. I tell it. There isn't much I know. Just the internet searches that I found and all the warning signs that I didn't heed. I track back through the history that binds me to my mother. I find it is all still sharp, all the little damages, death by a thousand cuts. When I finish talking I am exhausted by it. I feel like I have been bled out. I remember that my blood may have been used to keep Liv alive, each annual transfusion keeping death away from her door. If only my blood could do that for my own mother. Her blood is my blood and yet there is still no way for me to save her.

'And the terrible thing is it doesn't make me love her any more than I did before I knew.'

An awful admission. I bite my lip hard as if to punish my mouth for uttering it.

'Well.' L still hasn't let me out of the bear hug I am trapped in. My body is alive to L's body, I am aware of L's heartbeat, calm and steady inside L's bony chest. It settles me to listen to it, steady as a clock describing an eternity. 'I don't see why it would change anything. Well, not yet. All it has done is remind you that your relationship with your mother is temporal. You knew that. Now you have a shorter timeline. The way I see it you can change it if you want, but you can just keep on the same way. It isn't an imperative. Olivia is still the same person even if she's sick.'

'But shouldn't I feel, sad…or, I don't know. Something…?'

'You can if you want to. Or not. We are all in the process of dying. We each have our own schedule for it. That's all.'

L will die. I lie in the hug and I am aware of that coming

death as if it is a physical thing, a rope, circling L's heart, ready to pull tight and snuff out the regular pulse altogether. The way L describes it, it is just natural. No need to do anything but acknowledge that death is a part of life.

L will die. My mother will die. But first, and in a matter of weeks, Liv will die.

'Maybe,' L says, 'it's time to hurry things up with your mother. Pack all the years of one-sentence conversations into a shorter time.'

'Talk to her more?'

'Maybe.'

I hug L as close as I can. Our bodies are so tightly pressed together that we might as well be lovers, but we are not. My brand new body, which I have only explored through surface contact. In one hundred and ten years I too will be teetering on the edge of life as Liv is now. Every night that passes might be her last night.

L's breathing deepens. Those brown arms grow limp, L rolls away, presenting me with a back, the shirt pulled up, a sliver of chocolatey skin winking at me. I look at that patch of skin. I want to lick it. I am as far from sleep as I have ever been.

I roll off the mattress and make my way to the bathroom. I squat over the pot and listen to the sound of my piss hitting the metal. There is a mushroom growing out of the wall under the sink. Or a toadstool, I don't really know the difference. I watch the curl of it, ridged underneath like the belly of the whale in the ocean dome, liver-spotted like Liv's delicate skin. I lift my wrist to my mouth and I whisper, 'Text Liv Harbison.' I pause, not sure what I should say. I was wondering if you want to meet me for lunch...Another pause. A day might be like a year to her. Each morning brings the possibility of death. Tomorrow, I say, adding, if you're not already busy.

Her answer buzzes in my head almost immediately. I thought she might be asleep; I didn't expect to hear back from her so soon.

I'm supposed to be working tomorrow but fuck it, I'll wag.

I send her the address and the time. I take the pot to the window and tip it out. A few metres down my piss bleeds out into the river. Just a drop in the ocean, as they say. I think of all the run-off, all the chemical waste, all the dirt flushed out of abandoned buildings every time it floods. Every time I scramble out of the boat my ankles get red and itchy. There is a reason these buildings are condemned. There is a reason my mother hates me sleeping over with L.

When I climb into bed L is just a warm sack of flesh and bone. Absent, not here with me at all. If L were to die right now—this body, here, growing steadily colder—would the mind just drift off into the dream L is in now? Would the L I know and love continue to be L...incorporeally?

I hug L close and let the warmth of a living, breathing body spread across mine. Our equally ungendered bodies in lock step with each other, L's breath, my breath, L's heartbeat my heartbeat. And soon I will join L's consciousness, tangled in sleep.

*

The dying woman settles at the table opposite me. I dreamed of death, waking, gasping, clutching at the warm body beside me, then plunging down into even more death. I dreamed my consciousness existed in the earth where my skull had been buried. All I could feel was dampness. All I could see were the articulated soft bodies of worms that had taken up residence inside my skull. One of the worms asked me if I knew that it could reproduce asexually. I woke with my head throbbing, a slither in my ears, which may just have been the lapping of the river at the window of the unit below.

'I have no appetite,' she says to me, almost crossly. 'Food used to be a pleasure.'

She has ordered a salad and a glass of wine. None of my friends are drinkers. L doesn't touch the stuff. I hesitated before ordering a glass of wine for myself. Now it has arrived I wonder if it was a mistake. One, two sips and I am feeling light-headed already.

'You said you're still working?'

'Oh god, yes,' she says. 'I'll work till the day I drop, and longer. I'll need the cash.'

I frown, but it would be rude to ask about her debts.

'Gene therapy for this and for that. I have a pill box the size of a handbag,' she offers. 'Still, can't complain. Lucky to be a rich white Australian, right?'

All of her comments feel barbed. I am not sure if she is having a go at me for being rich.

'This gender thing is a final indulgence, I suppose. If I

make it to the middle. I am beginning to think I won't.'

'I'd be so frightened.'

She nods.

'I'm practising for a couple of hours a day but I'll never be ready for it.'

'Practising for death?'

She laughs. 'Yes. Long story. It is more complicated than you might expect.'

Liv picks at her salad. She places a lettuce leaf on her tongue and holds it in her mouth for a moment before chewing.

'I will miss eating. I will miss flavour the most. They didn't think of eating when they prepped for the afterlife. Tasting is something we will not be able to replicate for quite a while. Did you know an octopus tastes with all of its body? The ones that are left, that is.'

'You talk as if maybe you won't die.'

'Oh no. I'll die. But maybe, if it works, something of me will live on. It won't be me, because I'm inseparable from my body. But it will be a soft echo of who I was. In theory I will remember.' She stares off towards the busy street outside. I see her chest rise and hold for a long moment before she exhales. 'Or it won't work out the way it does with rats and I'll be completely gone, or worse, I'll be a monstrous version of myself.'

'You know you're going to have to explain all this to me now.'

She nods and smiles and I feel tight in my chest again.

There's that leap in my groin and I can feel the distribution of blood shifting.

'I am. I want to. Even now, when I've outlived everyone I love, I feel the need to confess. Isn't it silly?'

'What do you mean, something will live on? Are they going to keep you alive on a machine?'

'You could say that. But there's flesh in it too. It's called wetware, like a human brain. That's the best medium for the quantum probabilities of consciousness. I won't have a whole body either. They tried it—lucky I wasn't dead in time for *that* debacle. I'll just be something like a brain, getting on with my day job. Making ends meet…I wonder where that phrase came from? Well, no "ends" for this old boiler. Just more work. They only want me for my brain, you know.'

'And your body...?'

She moves her finger across her neck as if to slice her head off. She laughs. 'We are all dying. I will be dead soon. Weeks, probably. A month at most. And there is so much I didn't do.'

I have finished my pie. I have finished my wine. Her little plate of leaves is almost empty.

'Come on.'

I stand and run to the till and swipe my chip before she can protest.

'Where are we going?'

'To do something neither of us has ever done before.'

She grins and picks up her bag and wavers to her feet, a little unsteadily before finding her balance. I rush to her side and hold out my arm for her to take. She takes my hand instead and her fingers intersect with mine.

'Great,' she says, grinning. 'I knew you would be good fun. I knew it the moment I saw you in the clinic.'

'Ready for an adventure?'

'One last adventure,' she says. 'Let's do it.'

Our swimming pool is pretty beautiful. I know it, but I have always resented it. None of my other school friends had a pool and if they did it was just a communal pool for the whole building to share, a three-metre stretch of blue tiles with some tepid water in it. Our pool is landscaped to look like a rock pool. There are chiselled slabs of slate around the edges, the delicate curl of ferns. Because we are in the penthouse we have twice as much space as everyone else and the pool takes up half of it. The water is chilled so that even in the height of summer it is a refreshing change from the relentless heat of the day.

I take my clothes off. I do it in one hit so that I can't change my mind about it. I stand before her and I try to feel nothing but pride as I feel her looking at the unusual configuration of my parts. She stares. Her eyes scan the length of me. She seems curious about all of it, and not just my genitals. She looks at each of my toes, the bony ankles, the skinny calves. She doesn't flinch when she gets to my genitals. She takes them in, lingering over what might be my penis, or not, and then stretching her gaze up towards my stomach, my flat chest, my armpits, my neck.

'My mother said she won't be home till dark,' I tell her, and she nods.

'I thought we might swim.'

'Just swim?'

I feel the flush start at my chest and work its way up my throat, pinking the skin into blotches.

'No,' I tell her. 'I thought we would start by swimming.'

'And after that?'

'If something else happens you might remember it after your body dies.'

'Yes. Or I might not.'

I can feel the itchy red blotches staining my cheeks. I put the back of my hand to my face and feel the heat of it.

'Is this a parting gift to me, M? A gift for the dying?'

I try to calm my breathing. Maybe this was a mistake; I feel nothing but embarrassment.

'I haven't done it before,' I tell her. I am embarrassed by this, but it is the truth.

'What?'

'Any of it.' I want nothing more than to dive into the water and swim to the safe overhang of rocks but I stand my ground. I try to match Liv in her honesty.

'Sex?'

I nod.

'You have never had sex?'

Again a nod.

She looks away from me then. She stops to consider the careful landscaping. There is a little shrub with tiny pink flowers on it and her eyes move to the pretty branches as she considers.

'And you want to know what it's like?'

My head is on a spring, nodding up and down like an idiot.

'You might want to rethink that decision,' she says, and then she unclips the fastenings on her jumpsuit and lets it fall in a heap around her boots. She lifts the shirt carefully over her head, her short hair catches on the fabric and when her shirt is on the ground her hair is sticking up in erratic clumps. She is standing in her bra and pants. It is a push-up bra, I notice, and she unsnaps it at the front and when she takes it off her breasts nestle down and flatten against the bones of her chest. The nipples are pulled tight like two little pebbles, hard and dark on the paper-thin skin. She bends and slips her underpants down over her hips and she still has a prominent vulva. She has only just begun transitioning and all I can see of it is a slight protuberance where her clitoris has swelled into a little thumb. The swelling indicates that she (this body is still feminine, after all) is aroused. The lips of the vulva are thick and protruding, but that might be the gene therapy beginning to work. Still, she looks ready for sex. She looks up for it. Even the drape of that translucent skin folding over her hips cannot distract from what appears to be arousal.

'Look at me,' she says. 'See this body? Worn out.'

'Not yet.' I take a step towards the pool. I put my foot on the first slate step. The water is cool and soothing on the ball of my foot. 'Is it too much to ask?'

'Ask?' She exhales sharply. 'You don't have to beg me to have sex with a beautiful young body like yours. Look at you.'

And she is looking at me. She is watching me take slow steps down the stairs and into the sweet cool of the water. She watches as my genitals touch the surface; the water slowly flows around the vulva, kissing it like an icy mouth, then the cock, my little almost-cock, which slips into the water, hard as an arrowhead, filled up with the blood of my rising desire. The truth is I do desire her. This surprises even me now that I am confronted with her vulva at eye level. The folds of her skin there look like the curls of a paper nautilus. Her skin is that luminous jellyfish pale. She is a creature right out of the ocean and when she walks the little distance to the stone steps I follow her footfalls. I see the effort it takes for her to lift her feet out of her heavy boots. When her feet are as naked as the rest of her I watch her place each gnarled foot carefully. Her feet are like the roots of an old tree, misshapen, unsteady on the ground, pulling away from it in places and plunging towards it in others. She reaches the stairs and loses balance. I rush towards her in case she falls, but she steadies herself and she is climbing down towards me. Naked, wizened, proud. I raise my arms and she walks into them. She is butterfly soft. She crumples against me. She smells faintly of flowers, of an old lady's garden, heritage blooms.

I want her. I do want her. To be honest I want anyone, but she is here and I like her and it might just be happening. My first time might be happening. I have to remind myself to be gentle. She is a delicate flower that I might crush with my ardour. I can feel the swelling, hot in the cold water. I reach for her hand and she lets me take it and I place it against the throb at my groin. Her fingers curl around it. I thrust forward. I hold myself back, but it feels too good and I press my hips forward again. She stumbles and I hold her upright. She is a fragile collection of bones. I need to be careful with her. I am afraid I might kill her.

'I'm not sure what to do,' I tell her, surprised by the change in my voice; it has become raspy, deep, like I have been standing too close to an open fire.

'Let's go all the way into the water,' she says. 'It will do some work for me, support my body.' And she holds my shoulders and walks with me into the shallow end. We lean back together against the moss-covered bank. I can feel her chest trembling.

'Are you cold?'

'Nervous,' she says. 'I haven't done this for quite a while.'

I feel her fingers back on me, circling me and one finger of her left hand gently exploring my swollen vulva. She finds the space between the lips. I can feel how slippery I am. Her finger slides easily inside. She tests the tightness of my hymen. I push forward, taking her finger deeper into me, making her hand slide around the shaft at the same time.

'I really want to put my mouth on you,' she says. 'I want to remember what it tastes like.'

I groan. The image of her taking my clitoris into her mouth, the heft of it stretching her lips, flashes into my mind and I feel a quick lurch in my groin. I groan a second time and press back into her grip a few more times, pumping myself into the palm of her hand, enjoying the way it makes her finger slip up and down inside me. 'I could get up on the edge. Then you could take me in your mouth.'

'Soon,' she says. Touches a second finger to the lips of my vulva, wiggles it back and forth until it slips inside. I feel myself stretched out as far as my hymen will allow. I push forward again. I want it broken. I want more of her in me. I think of her little swollen clitoris. In a few weeks it will be big as two fingers, maybe fat as three. It would feel like this if she were to put it inside me. We could take turns. Her in me. Me in her.

I know what I want now. I gently push her hands away and I hug her to me. Her nipples rub against mine as I walk her back against the bank. I carefully hold the cheeks of her arse in my hands. Jellyfish skin. It ripples against my fingers. I lift her and she is light as a piece of tissue billowing up with the movement of the water. I rest her down against me, shift my hips from side to side and her thighs float upward, exposing her to the press of me. I gently ease her down and my eyes close as her cunt closes around me. In her and out of her and in her again. Warm and cold. Alive and dead. Alive. I press up into her. I am in her. I have to be sure; I move one of my hands to where our bodies have melted together and I follow the tip of my penis-clit as it pushes up into her again. I fumble with the soft folds of her genitals. I can feel myself pumping into her. One of my fingers touching the base of my protrusion, one of them slipping into the thick viscosity of my own cunt and I feel myself begin to pulse around my own finger. Each pulsation forces me higher up into her body. Her extended clitoris is rubbing gently against the thatch of hair on my pubic bone. I feel her tilt her body slightly and bounce there. I am in and out, in and out until the excitement subsides in my own body but she is still bouncing there on top of my deflated member. I give her my finger instead, slicked as it is with my own excitement. She pushes hard against my pubis, she presses down onto my hand, and there it is, that jellyfish propulsion, that wave of pleasure and her nipples clipping harder against my chest as she comes. We float in the rise and fall of the water for a long while. We say nothing. Her arms around me, my arms around the brittle body that she is living in.

After what seems an age she says, 'I want you to sit on the edge now.'

'Yeah?' I can feel the excitement building already.

'I want you all over my face.'

These words must be the most exciting thing anyone has ever said to me. I am half out of the water already. I am making towards the stairs.

'I'll do it to you next,' I say as I slide down onto the mossy bank and let my feet push down into the water, feet like hands pulling her close.

'You don't have to,' she says.

'Are you kidding? Why wouldn't I want to do that?'

Then there are her lips, and her tongue, and her lips and tongue and her fingers and the palm of her hand and more fingers and they are in me and slipping in places I would never have imagined. She is good at this. I suppose that's what happens with so many years of practice, but there is something else too. She wants me. I can tell by the way she puts her lips around me. She is hungry for me, or for my youth, or for the memory of her youth. Whatever it is, it is working for me. I lie back on the rocks and I lift my hips a little so she can get into all the places. At one point I push down on her fingers, I reach down and stuff three of them into me. I want my hymen gone. She pulls her hand away.

'It's going to hurt you,' she says. 'I don't want you to associate what we did here with pain. She takes her finger out and it is wet with me and I feel her lubing up the other hole and she bobs forward and opens her mouth and takes my whole cock in between her wet lips and when I blow I might be ejaculating into her mouth like a man, or pulsing like a woman and it doesn't really matter because she holds on with her lips and strokes with her tongue and her fingers and it feels like all of my body has gone into and through her so that even the muscles in my shoulders are pumping my life force down into the rocks and the dirt.

I sit up and grin at her and she is grinning back. I can't believe that it is happening. I grab a handful of reeds in each hand just to know that I am here and we are doing this right now. It all feels so solid. I feel so alive.

'Now you.'

'Only if you want to,' she tells me. 'I don't need…'

And then I am submerged. I plunge down to the bottom of the pool, hold my breath, push my face up to the delicate flesh between her legs. My lips part and I take her little cock into my mouth, I rub it with my tongue and it gets bigger. One day, if she makes it to centre, it will be as big as mine. I want it inside me. I want it in my cunt, but for now my mouth will have to do.

My tongue in her, around her, in her. My fingers stroking her. There is a scar, a pale line across her upper thigh and I kiss it while I push my finger inside her. She doesn't have the same lubrication that my body makes so naturally and so I put my hand between my own legs and scoop up my own juices, which I push inside her. There is spit and there is vaginal juice and there is soft nautilus flesh and there is nothing but her in my face.

I open my eyes to sex. I blow bubbles up into it and have to surface to take another quick gasp of air before going back to the cave to play. If I laugh under the water she will not hear me. If I speak her name into her own orifice there is nothing but the tickle of air in water. If I tilt my body I can bring my reinvigorated cock up between her legs for a quick push inside her. I am in her and around her and I can feel her excitement building. It is in the way she moves, the sudden roughness of her fingers grabbing at my hair. I am quick with my hand and my tongue and she comes into my palm and around my tongue and into my mouth and around my finger and I laugh up into her cunt. My bubbles of joy. I have never felt more like myself. I have never abandoned self-awareness in quite this way. When she finishes her orgasm I burst to the surface of the water, gasping and laughing, and there is her mouth, thrown open and the squeal of her laughter is like some sound an animal might make, the pure scream of pleasure.

'Thank you,' we say at exactly the same time, then we laugh and hug and thank each other with our voices and our hands and our mouths. I feel the buzz at my wrist of a message coming through but I ignore it the first time. A second buzz and I am panting, but I reluctantly let the message seep into my consciousness.

Darling—my mother—do you think you could come over to the hospital? In your own time. No hurry.

We are somewhere on the journey towards death.

I hold my mother's hand while she vomits. I don't suppose I will ever get used to the violence of this purging. I shift uncomfortably on the plastic chair. Liv was right. It did hurt. But I don't mind the sting of it. I am glad I got to feel her swelling so big inside me. At one point, lying beneath me, pushing up as hard as she could, before the tearing of flesh and the sharp pain of it, she stopped; panting, coughing a little, obviously straining to complete the act. 'I might go all the way to the other side,' she said. 'Do you think? What kind of a man would I make?'

I looked down into her sweet, sweating face. I felt my heart and my cunt stretching wider and wider around her. 'You would make a really beautiful man.' I said it, and I meant it. Her age is nothing to me anymore. I was staring down through her skin. I was staring at what would be left when the flesh was gone and I saw her. That's when it happened, at the moment I saw her, the beauty of her. I winced and the flesh tore and I bled onto her new little cock and slipped lower and closer to her and she knew she had done it but she couldn't help herself. She had been close and that slight slip, up further into me, set her off and I watched her face change with the consummation of her pleasure and I knew something new. It was a calmness. A peace. It would be all right.

I hold my mother's hair back from her face. It is coming out in patches but she won't let me shave it off.

My mother and I have resolved nothing. I wait till her breathing returns to normal. I look at her face, which is similar but different to my face. We will never completely resolve everything that is bad between us, but L was right. We are coming to terms with each other. In that way this has brought us closer.

I send the text to Liv again and she is still not answering. I had such a lovely morning. Thank you.

But the words float out into the void, unheard.

I know she is dead, or transferred. She said it would be soon, so I suppose it has happened. A few weeks ago I would have been inconsolable but now I just feel like it is the way things have to be.

My wrist buzzes, but it isn't Liv.

Where are you? L asks.

Hospital.

Need some company?

Want, I reply, not need. But want.

Glad you want me. L is teasing. We both know that L's definition of 'want' is something different from the way I might use it. I'll be over in a few minutes.

'L's coming round,' I tell my mother.

She nods.

'Are you sleeping with L yet?'

'Don't you dare say that when L is here.'

'I won't. You know I won't.'

I know she won't.

'But I still think you should be.'

'I'm happy with L,' I tell her. 'For now I am happy.'

'But I want you to experience passion, sexual passion. It really is wonderful, M. Believe me. There is nothing else like it.'

I clamp my knees together. I feel the sharp pain of the tear which has not yet healed. I smile. A little sad smile that lingers on my lips for the longest time. She is right. For once my mother and I are in agreement. But I say nothing to her. I just hold the bowl close by because there is always a second wave of nausea. When it comes I will be ready for it.

PART 5
LIV

I AM BEAUTIFUL.

I have never before been beautiful and this first glimpse of this body in the mirror startles me. That was not part of the deal. I didn't even think about the aesthetic dimension. Male, Female, Ungendered. These were my choices. I ticked the box out of habit. Easier to continue as I was for most of my past; and yet I did not expect this.

It is difficult to believe that someone who looks like this does sex work. The world is still so kind to the beautiful, even more so than when I was a kid. This woman could charm her way into any job and yet here she is.

Is it okay if you turn around? I ask. She sees the words, or perhaps she hears them, as if they have been cut loose from her thoughts to echo in her skull, but there is no real sound.

She turns. A slow reveal of a waist that is nipped in neatly, a tight, high arse, an elegantly curved back. When she comes back around to the front I see her breasts again. The nipples are very pale and very pink. Her breasts seem too heavy for so slight a frame. They sway a little when she turns but they are firm, pert, the nipples pointing upwards. Perhaps she has had some work done, made them bigger and higher. If she has I can't tell. They seem just as soft and pliant as the rest of her.

'Do you want me to turn around again?' she asks out loud.

Hahaha my laughter is translated to the actual word like letters on a screen, I can feel the shape of it. This also surprises me. I smile, imagining the software developer who decided to subtitle this emotional response as well. Liv smiles—I wait for the letters to form in our shared consciousness, but no. There is just the feeling of smiling and I doubt that it is something she shares.

Her name is Laura. She works as a prostitute. She prefers the archaic term for it, because that is what she put on her profile. Laura. Prostitute. Twenty-three. Female.

Yes. She is indeed female.

You are beautiful, I tell her, and now she smiles along with me. It feels good to smile, to really smile with skin that tightens and lifts. To match a mouth to the way I am feeling. She flicks her long blonde hair away from her shoulder and I feel it brushing against her skin.

'Thank you,' she says.

You don't have to speak aloud, I remind her.

Thank you, she says without words.

I am paying for eight hours of her life each week. The

numbers are there in the corner of my mind, the seconds ticking over. I have already used ten minutes of her time.

I need to feel the space your body takes up, I tell her. I still feel disembodied.

Do you want me to have sex? she asks.

No. Nothing like that, I say too quickly. I am not quite ready for that. I am still remembering what it is to be in the world. Would you take a bath?

She scowls. It is an automatic response, this ugly impatience marring her exceptional face. I'm not sure I would have liked her if I were not here inside her, but she is all I have for now.

'You want me to take a bath?'

If that's okay.

She shrugs. 'I'm on the clock.'

I remember everything. I remember the smell of bubble bath. I used to use a brand called Relax, from Herb Farm. It smelled of the ocean. She uses a sharper scent, cheap, but even this minor assault on the senses is a pleasure. I drink in the heady waft. The smell is being filtered in through her experience, and it's strange to smell something through someone else. I know it is a smell that would have irritated me when I had my own body to experience it through. Her sense of smell seems different, though. The edges of it dulled.

I didn't realise how strange this would seem. She tests the water with her fingers, the sweet, thick resistance warm, honey-like. She lifts her leg. She steps easily into the tub.

In my old body I never trusted myself to climb into a bath

like this. Even when I was young I would hold on to the towel rail. My legs were stiff, my balance unreliable. I had one too many mishaps with soapy water and clean tiles. She is sure-footed as a heron, her limbs long and steady. She curls herself into the bath and I am there with her. I find the edges of myself through the water. The hug of warmth defines the body, makes me suddenly three-dimensional. I feel unreasonably long and thin. I feel snakelike.

I try to move my arm but there is nothing except a twitch of her index finger. I strain to stretch my left leg out; for the longest time there is no response. I am exhausted by the effort of will. I concentrate all of myself on that single limb and then it shifts, stretches.

She shifts it back into her body. 'Fuck,' she says out loud.

Did I just move your leg?

'That's so weird,' she says.

You don't need to speak out loud.

'Do it again,' she says aloud and I am tempted to use my mother's words. 'Inside voice!' I want to shout. But I don't. This must be just as strange for her as it is for me.

'Pick up the soap,' she tells me, gripping the side of the bath. There is no way I can override her resistance.

I can't do it when you try to stop me.

'I suppose that's a good thing.'

I nod. And she is nodding.

Was that me? Or you?

'A bit of both, I think.' Then she picks up the soap and rubs it against our stomach and it feels like I'm sliding through thick sweet cream. She rubs the soap against her breasts and the sensation is sublime. I feel my agency melt away. I am relaxing into her hands.

'Do you want me to masturbate?' she asks me, but she doesn't wait for me to answer. She is already slipping the soap down between her legs, sliding the hardness of it across her hairless vulva. I am reduced to my senses as she expertly slips a finger into the soapy slit, rubbing small circles around her clitoris. She is good at this. Well, it is her job, I suppose.

It strikes me now that this is the first time I have paid for the services of a prostitute, and I guess that makes me her trick. If this were one of my narratives I would begin here.

The first time I paid a prostitute to masturbate me was when my body had died. I was nothing more than a collection of thought patterns, memories stored digitally, circuits firing like synapses, and yet this woman was slipping her fingers up and inside me.

It would be a good story, an incorporeal story about corporeality. The possibilities excite me, but as soon as I have thought it, I let it go. I spend every waking hour thinking; always thinking. Now it's time to let a body lead me. She slips a second finger into us, eases down further into the bath and stretches her elongated hand further still, teasing my, her, bottom with the perfectly manicured pink nail of her little finger. Three more circles of her thumb and I am not sure if the groan that escapes her mouth issues from me or from her.

*

Can you fake an orgasm when your lover is inside your brain?

I should be thinking about my work but I am distracted. I have languished in an echo chamber of memory all morning. I have been remembering the times when my body pressed itself against a lover's flesh. I keep thinking about the way I like someone to kiss the back of my neck, how it sparks goosebumps all over my skin, makes my vulva clench with pleasure. Next time I'm inside her I want her to have sex. I lose myself in a maze of this problem instead of writing the narrative that I am working on.

My own work seems paradoxical, I am a brain pattern busy scanning through the brain patterns of others, making sense of them, finding words to describe to others the story that emerges. A brain viewing a brain, and yet I remember my body so clearly, more intensely now that I have piggy-backed inside someone else's flesh.

I force myself to concentrate on the job I'm doing but this thought keeps returning. Did she really have an orgasm? Or was she pretending? Was it just me who came, while she expertly sent her compliant body through the motions? Isn't that what sex workers do?

I clock off. I am too distracted for work. I will rest now, think my way through my own conundrum before trying to concentrate on someone else. I sink into a resting state and this is what I needed. A little nap. Some time to immerse myself in memory. Her long pink-nailed hands, her sweet soft fingers, the sharp scent of bubble bath, the orgasm that came and came and came again. She wouldn't let it drift off into nothing as I always used to do, she kept me there, endlessly tumbling over myself till the hour was up and it was time for me to log out of her body and let her go back to whatever else she does in her own real life.

Can a sex worker fake her orgasm when someone else is inside her brain? That is the question that won't let me relax into sleep. I nap and wake, enervated. Eventually I log in to a new file. I think the words and they appear on the empty virtual page: The first time I paid a prostitute to masturbate me was when my body had died.

I have paid for six more hours this week. Starting this evening. I am aware of each slow second as I type the words describing what happened. I should be typing someone else's story. I should be earning the money to pay the exorbitant cost of my body-worker, but instead, for the first time since I stopped writing memoir in my thirties, I am busy typing up my own.

Laura takes me to a club. We wait in a long and sweaty queue. Her arm brushes the sequined back of a young woman. The feel of it, the sequins, the catching of flesh, all this is so sharp and focused that it would be enough. I would spend my five hours just here waiting in the queue having Laura brush up against one body after another and I would have spent my money well. This is what it is to have a body. I remember the feel of my skin dampening. The slow trickle of water carefully tracking the line of my shoulders and pooling at my waist.

I was never the nightclub kind of girl, even in my youth.

The other students would spend each Friday and Saturday evening dancing to some band, pressed up against strange flesh, flirting and finding someone to end up holding their hair as their body heaved over a toilet bowl.

I would take my things and head home. Studying, finishing assignments, reading the set texts; one day very similar to another. This proximity of skin, this heady mix of pheromones sharp in my nostrils: this is what I was missing out on.

Laura has a body that gets noticed in a queue. The men are looking at her, their glances feel like moths. She is aware of their attention, or I am. I suppose it is the same. We turn our body a little when this man or that looks in our direction. I suppose she is using her body to encourage them. These subtle movements, flicking the hair away from our face, shifting her weight to one hip to set our torso at an angle, pulling her shoulders back and the burgeoning of flesh that happens when she does that. Our nipples are erect, poking through the thin fabric of her shirt, and this is something to watch. We are watched.

The queue creeps forward but we are still a dozen people from the entry. A man in a red shirt open at the collar walks past the row of damp, bright-eyed people. He sweeps the column as if picking out a criminal from a line-up. He stops beside Laura. His gaze takes in the soft silver drape of her shirt, the fabric clinging to all the rising and falling-away of flesh, the prick of nipples clearly visible, held in place by the most diaphanous of undergarments. He looks at the short kick of her skirt and the stretch of stockinged legs beneath. I have never been looked at this way and it excites me. I feel the rush of damp slicking our vulva. I am sure this excitement is mine and not hers. There is no point trying to untangle one of us from the other because I am knitted into her senses. I am a part of the weave of her brain pattern. This kind of scrutiny excites me, and therefore she is excited.

He holds out his arm towards us and I hesitate, but that impulse is far less strong than Laura's firm reach forward to take hold of the crook of his arm. The red shirt is made of some sort of stiff cotton. My fingers rub back and forth over it, taking in the rough weave, toying with the folds of fabric before Laura purposefully makes a fist to stop my fingers. She is familiar with the role we must play in these circumstances and she takes over. It is a little like being a passenger in a car: watching the road ahead, anticipating the moves we will make, and every so often the driver takes her hands off the wheel and lets me take control.

She is driving now, though, as we are plucked from the impatient queue and ushered towards the bright lights framing the door to the club.

The bouncer is dressed in a shirt slightly too small for the bulk of his muscles. He smells gamey, like aged meat, as we brush past him. The red-shirted man nods, and smiles are exchanged before he is waved through into a sudden wall of sound.

You should ask his name.

This is my habitual politeness speaking. I am uncomfortable when the niceties are not exchanged. I can feel her thought-smile; her mouth remains a crimson pout. Then her voice comes clear and loud, cutting through the thumping of the music.

His name isn't important. Just wait. There will be other men tonight. We can pick whichever we want. You choose. It's your night.

It takes a moment for my eyes to adjust to the darkness of the room. It is seething with bodies, but in the smoky gloom it is hard to determine gender among the gyrating figures. I wonder for a moment if the room is filled with twilighters, and feel a small pang of nostalgia for my brief time with M.

When my eyes adjust, I realise my error: the revellers are all hypersexualised, like cartoon characters in a manga comic. The women are hyper-femme, squeezed into plunging dresses. Shimmering fabric is in this season and their beads and tassels catch the light and scatter it out to the edges of the dance floor. The men are all butch and top-heavy in their tight muscle shirts and thin cotton trousers.

It is hotter than I remember, if this is even possible. Each year the temperature climbs and the club uses this, letting the dancers stew in their sweat till they are hot and ripe. At the edges of the main room there are recessed booths and the chill air spills out of them like breath on a winter morning, the way I still remember from childhood. These booths are a place to cool down after the bacchanalian dancing. A place to ease oneself into the arms of strangers in full view of the sweating, surging crowd.

The man in the red shirt walks us straight to the bar and the waiter reaches across the other bodies to slip two drinks into his hands. He doesn't put his chipped wrist out to pay and I wonder what the arrangement is. Is he the owner of the bar? A friend of the owner? Someone famous I have failed to recognise?

Is it safe to drink? I ask Laura as she brings the glass to her lips.

Nothing is ever safe. Isn't that the wonder of having a body? Laura asks and this time when she laughs the sound, the stretch of laughter touches our actual lips. Red Shirt steers us towards a booth already occupied by six people, leaning into each other, hands resting on thighs resting on other thighs. A nest of restless young flesh all a-slither. A young man with a moustache shifts across to allow us to perch beside him. His knee is pressed up against Laura's thigh.

Red Shirt clicks his glass against mine and we are drinking. The alcohol burns warm and sweet down to the stomach. I raise the glass quickly back to our mouth but she pulls it away. She is taking the wheel again, easing my foot off the accelerator. She will not let me get drunk too quickly. Instead she lifts her face up to the man with the red shirt and he leans forward to kiss our lips. And I remember this. He reaches out with fingers cooled by his glass and slips them into the cowled neck of our shirt and pinches the nipple. Laura is too late to stifle my groan. He takes the little noise as a provocation and wraps his fingers around our breast. I want to open my mouth, to take his tongue against mine. I want all the sensation of flesh against, around and inside flesh but Laura's mouth remains firmly shut. She takes our hand and squeezes the man's crotch and I can feel how hard he is. She stands then and tilts her head to one side, blowing a kiss through the humid air.

'Thanks for the drink,' she says and then she walks us both away.

I have never been so desirable. It is probably best that Laura sticks to the same glass of warm gin; I am already drunk on the way men look at me. Their eyes describe my body to me. Without this constant attention it would be easy to forget I am in a different body now, as I kept doing yesterday in Laura's flat. She would walk past a mirror and there was her body instead of mine. Here in the bar it is just me, and all their eyes drawing a Laura-shaped line wherever I go.

Is it okay to have sex with one of them? I ask her and she turns our head to scan the room.

Which one would you choose?

I look past the dancing bodies to the standing drinking bodies to the seated caressing bodies. They are a different breed of people from the ones I've known in my real life. All the bespectacled men I spent time with, all the poets and coders and software developers, all the interactive filmmakers and the novelists experimenting with form. None of them looked as glossy or as fit as these people in this room. But then none of them ever looked quite the way this body I am in does now.

I don't really care, I tell her honestly. I don't really like any of them in particular. I just want to feel a body next to mine. How about you pick?

She presses out on to the dance floor and we are swaying to the music. I think it's up to you to pick, she tells me. It will be like musical chairs. We dance and then when the music stops…

But when her body starts to bounce to the pounding thud of the music I know that I won't ever want this particular dance to stop.

She is on top of him. She perches so easily on his lap. Her legs are longer than mine were and in this body it is easy to kneel over him and settle onto his lap.

The music stopped and he and Laura found themselves together. Okay. He isn't anyone I would have given a second glance in my real life, but he smells all right, like spiced after-shave. There are Celtic knots tattooing his upper arms, spreading when he stretches his muscles, the undulation of an ornate mobius strip. I would have drawn the line at a Southern Cross tattoo. If I'd had time—the transaction was over in a minute. She leaned forward, tall enough on her stilettos that she had to bend a little to speak directly into his ear.

'You want to come back to my place?'

And he did no more than nod.

So this, now, is what it feels like to slip down onto a firm young cock. I focus all of my attention on that one place, the opening and parting. The feeling of stretching, the chemical high of pure pheromone breathed in too quickly too deeply as she surges up and down. I let her do what she is doing without interference and for the first minute it is enough. I am in my body at last. I am truly at one with the flesh that I am in.

But there is no elevation of the rush. I need my clitoris engaged and the way she is bouncing is doing nothing for that sensitive part of our anatomy. I move her right hand to touch us. The gorgeous shock of stimulation. We tilt our head back and close our eyes. I make small beautiful circles.

'What—' she catches herself speaking aloud and thinks the words instead, *What are you doing?*

Pleasuring us.

It's strange that she had to ask. I pause, but she doesn't resist as I start the tiny circles again. The man is thrusting up too hard, too deep. I reach down with my left hand and wrap two fingers around his shaft, keeping his movements shallow, slowing his rhythm, thinking it's odd that Laura doesn't think to do this. And then, just as my arms are becoming sore and cramping up I feel the wave overtake me. I press my thumb hard against her clit and release his cock. Here in the last throes of the orgasm it doesn't really matter how hard or fast he moves. I am as soft and flexible as a rag doll and I let him roll me over so that he can pump into me with more vigour. He thrusts again and again and again and then he is jerking into her, shaking, losing his rhythm. I pull her knees up to my chest and roll away.

You do that? She manages the words, although I know she is winded, startled by the intensity of the orgasm we just shared.

Do what?

Isn't it rude to do yourself when you are with a man?

What?

Toss off …

We had sex.

Yes, but you were wanking. Taking care of yourself without any respect for him.

I … I just wanted to come. Don't you make yourself come when you are having sex?

Her silence is telling. I want to reach over and hug her curled body but I can't. It is our curled body. The man reaches over with one heavy, exhausted arm and tweaks our nipple instead.

Why do you have sex if you don't come?

If I'm working?

No. When you do it for pleasure.

I don't know. I go into the bathroom after and then I think about what we just did and then I try to come.

I vaguely remember that. Always too nervous to come during sex. Each new partner seemed overwhelming; I couldn't focus on the task. She isn't so unusual. And god, she's young. When I was her age I sometimes used to wait till afterwards myself.

Life's too short, I tell her now. If there's one thing I have learnt in one hundred and thirty years, it's that if you don't give yourself one nobody else will.

I feel ourselves blushing. The heat is rushing into our cheeks. A sex worker who is bashful. Maybe there are some benefits to aging. I have learnt to take what is not forthcoming; even in my short and unwieldy body I could give myself everything I wanted.

Didn't you like it? I ask.

Sure.

Do you want to do it again?

She rolls onto her other side and looks at the man. He is still young. Capable of taking us both one more time before my night in her body comes to an end.

Is it okay if I blow him? she asks me. Just to get him going again?

By all means. I have no problem giving head—as long as he gives back.

She shakes her head and leans down towards the full condom still dangling on his limp cock. She snaps it off and clumsily rolls a second one onto the wilting hang of flesh. When she puts her mouth on him I feel the blood expanding his cock between my lips.

For some reason, she says, I didn't expect someone as old as my grandmother to know her way around a man.

Well, if I was your grandmother I would tell you not to talk with your mouth full.

She laughs out loud but it is muffled as he pushes his swelling penis towards the back of our throat.

Slow down, cowboy, I say, but there is no way he could hear. I place her fist around the base of his cock again to stop him pushing so hard, and I can feel her awareness of my actions. She is watching my technique. She is taking it all in. I like that I can teach her something. I grin and suck, and touch myself a little at the same time. I still have at least an hour before time's up but I suspect she'll forgive me if we go a little overtime. She pulls our head away from him and licks her lips.

She is grinning cheekily as she tells him, 'Okay, cowboy'—my word, not hers—'now it's our turn. You ready to go down for some peach?'

She looks at the queue lining up for tickets. It's not the money that's bothering her, since I am paying the extra. It's the unfamiliarity of the venue. There will be no one here to pluck her from the line and ease her through in front of everyone else. Half the line is a rattle of children, hopping from one foot to the other, making sudden dashes out to press their hands and cheeks against the window, staring out at the fistfuls of hail pounding uselessly against the augmented glass. A little boy dances on the spot before rushing back to his father in the slowly progressing line. A girl of about seven thrusts her way through a series of set moves, judo classes perhaps, or tae kwon do. Laura watches her go through the careful mime, then put her head down and her arms out and aeroplane back to her mother, standing in front of us in the queue.

Laura takes a step back when she approaches. It is clear she hasn't had much to do with children. She turns and stares back at the rest of the people. Bookish girls with short green and pink bobs and a serious set to the mouth, hugging thick textbooks, standing firm in their heavy-soled boots. Boys with glasses and startled expressions who look permanently surprised to be alive at all. An ungendered person, small and slight with a lightly furred chin, perhaps caught mid-transition from the neutral space into male.

Laura quickly looks back towards the snaking line and clutches her handbag to her chest. She is wearing matching pink heels. She is long and lithe and beautiful and yet here, where no one seems to notice her, she has lost her position as something extraordinary. I can feel the small slump of her shoulders, the studied pout. She is here because she is being paid to take me here, but she would prefer to be at home.

The line creeps forward and the hail dwindles to heavy rain. We pay our money at the gate and I remember the man who takes our cash. His name is Herb, which is nice when you end up in the scented garden and imagine him eating his lunch on a break amid the rosemary and the thyme. She barely looks at him when he takes her money but I move her eyes back. I look. He seems tired, like he's slept badly.

Ask him how he is today.

'How are you today?'

He looks up at her for the first time. He almost smiles.

'Very well, thank you for asking.'

He gives her change and she smiles a little and he seems grateful for the smile, grinning back and opening the gate for her to walk through.

'The ten o'clock show is about to start,' he says. 'Oceans of the Past.'

I love that one. I've seen it but I love it. I smile again and we nod.

We sit in rows like a lecture theatre. Almost every seat is taken, which seems to surprise her, and we have to push past an Indian man with a neat glossy beard and an old lady with her hair tied severely back into a bun to get to the only free seat. There is a father and his child on the left side of us and a young man with a T-shirt that says *Plato's Cave: Search and Rescue Mission* on the front. I smile and her mouth makes the shape of it but I can tell she is baffled by my amusement.

She is as uncomfortable here as I was in her nightclub. She puts the headpiece on and looks from side to side. The child is jiggling up and down, thumping down onto his hands, which he rests beneath him. The Search and Rescue man is shy and quiet at her other side. He smells like smoke. It is as if he has come straight from warming his hands at an open fire and I wonder what he was doing before his trip to the planetarium. Forestry perhaps. Maybe he was just at home, burning off debris from the last storm.

We start the experience in water. It happens quickly and unexpectedly, and even though I have been waiting for the show to begin I am, as always, surprised by it. The tiny fish dart between our fingers and she feels them flicking silvery, nibbling at the skin of her elbow and so I feel it too. It is a strange piggybacking. She is imagining these fish are real. They are created directly in her neural pathways. She senses them as clearly as she senses the man beside her holding his hands up to let the fish slip against his palms. Her own senses are tricking her into believing that the whole space is filled with schools of fish. And here I am, my own senses fooling me into believing I can feel her hands reaching up to brush a fish away from her cheek. I feel the slip of its scales, the cool weight of it, the way its muscular body adjusts and finds its place in the school. Layer upon layer upon layer of deception and yet this is all we are, this filtered interaction with the world. I am in her body therefore I have a body. Her body.

I remember fish, I tell her, real fish.

No way.

I am one hundred and thirty years old. When I was a kid I used to go fishing in the ocean. With a rod and bait, and we didn't know how rare a thing that would be in just a few years.

I can feel her wonder. She puts out her hands and there are bigger fishes now to stroke and turn in our imaginary water. A large angelfish darts past and she reaches across to touch it and the man beside us reaches at the same time and our hands link. We have missed the fish entirely but here we are, our fingers locked together and we look at each other's faces for the first time and I see that his eyes are heavy lidded and very brown. I notice his skin, dark and buttery and even his fingers in my hand feel soft. I smell an open fire and the hidden sweetness of soap beneath. He has balanced a satchel of books on his lap; I can see the corner of one peeking out and I know the image on the jacket. I have that same edition, or I used to.

I reluctantly let go of his fingers and smile, nodding down into his lap. '*We Have Always Lived in the Castle?*' The words come out of her mouth seamlessly. My thoughts, her words. She no longer feels like a car that I am driving. She feels like me. I am the car, and I ease myself out into the oncoming traffic.

He is nodding.

'I love that book,' I tell him. 'I always felt that she was me, you know? That I lived in that castle. That book felt like it described me exactly.'

'Yeah,' he says. 'I know what you mean. That scene at the beginning when she walks into the shop? To be honest, that's about as far as I've got but I love it already.'

I laugh and then I flinch, hold my hands up in front of my face to ward off the big graceful shadow of the shark. He laughs and reaches out to touch the sandpapery skin.

'I can't get used to sharks,' I tell him. 'I still get scared they are going to eat me with all those teeth.'

'That's crazy.'

'When—' but the words are taken away from me. Laura has closed her lips and keeps them tight shut.

When I was a girl? she asks silently. *Really? Are we going to tell him your fishing stories?*

And I know she's right. I can't go around telling everyone that I'm just a collection of neural patterns. No flesh left, just a jumble of quantum probabilities.

'What?' he asks and balances a cuttlefish on the palm of his hand.

'When this is done,' Laura continues for me, 'do you want to go get something to eat?'

She startles both of us with her suggestion. I can see him backing away, cautious. He is not used to a strange woman asking him out on a date. I am not used to asking someone. He and I have both been ambushed by her superior confidence with men. The hesitation is only momentary. He begins to smile cautiously as he nods.

'I would love to. Actually.'

'Oh. Octopuses,' I say, pointing, and Laura seems to disappear from my consciousness as I point and feel a single tentacle wrap around my finger, the suckers tasting her flesh, or pretending to taste because it isn't real. It is imaginary and yet it is tasting her skin. I am probably not real either and yet I feel the press of his knee against mine. She has encouraged him and I don't pull away from the warmth of his leg. I wish I had done this more often when I had a body, I could have just come to the planetarium and watched the fishes and picked up some strange, sweet boy. But I was too old. For so much of it I was just too old. I doubt that this boy would have pressed his warm leg against my wizened old flesh. By the time I was old enough to know what I wanted, the men I wanted, I was too old to be attractive to them.

I am in Laura's body now and she is more beautiful than I ever was. It would be such a sweet surprise for someone who looks like her to be at all interested in someone as bookish as this young man now.

When the blue whale lumbers gently through the water overhead we both look up and his fingers find mine. The pressure of his hand seems right. We watch the sky and there is a leviathan passing overhead and I remember that time in my father's fishing boat. How old was I? Ten, maybe? I remember the sound, a huffing coming out of nowhere. I remember my father switching the engine off and drifting, open mouthed, and I didn't know what we were waiting for until the whale surfaced, not close enough to touch but even at that distance it seemed magical. A southern right whale, and my dad reaching for my hand and the two of us just bobbing in the boat watching the slow curl of its dark body rising above the surface of the ocean. I felt a little wave of fear because it wasn't close enough to knock our boat over but maybe if it dived down and surfaced one more time it would be. Still, even with that shudder of worry I felt the excitement too.

The whale disappeared and we waited in the silence but it never surfaced again. I wasn't disappointed. I had never seen a whale that close before and it was a new and wonderful thing. My father kept holding my hand for the longest time and when he finally let me go to start the motor of the little boat I set my mouth in a firm line and told him that I was going to be a marine biologist when I grew up.

'Good,' he said. 'But you have to do well at maths and science if you are going to do that.'

'I will,' I said. A turning point. One of the few in my life that I remember clearly. I didn't study fish but I still love them, even now when there are no whales left in the oceans and hardly any fish at all. When I had a body I would go down to the sea and watch the swarm of jellyfish bob at the surface, and remember.

The whale passes over and is gone. The boy lets go of my hand and I feel the disappointment of both these things.

'I'm Liv,' I tell him and then I hear the sharp tut from my

mouth and it is Laura, but he doesn't seem to notice.

'I'm Anthony,' he says, and he finds my hand again, this time to shake it as we acknowledge our first formal introduction.

'Pleased to meet you.'

'Likewise.'

His fingers curl up with mine on the arm of the chair between us. We are holding hands. Openly.

I feel a slight unease. It is just like when my father and I saw the whale breaking the surface. It was the size of the beast, the beauty of it, something about its immensity that made me frightened, knowing how easy it would be to capsize.

I feel this now. The potential for a fall. The threat is not immediate; we are safe at the moment. The whale is still a little way off. The water is undulating, but at this point relatively still. I hold on to Anthony's hand and I feel as if this boat we are in is precarious. *If you fall in the water in winter you have minutes*, my father used to tell me. *That's out there*—pointing. *You have to get yourself back into the boat quick smart. If the sharks don't get you then the cold sure will.*

I feel a small shiver tracing the line of my spine. I grip his fingers more tightly. They feel warm. Real, more than the dancing or even the sex. His body feels like a small anchor and holding his hand here under the impossible ocean I feel like I am finally coming to rest after a long time of drifting about unmoored.

*

I still need sleep. This has been a surprise. I have taken on more work, but I find that I will be working on one problem or another and there is a sudden slowing. If I were corporeal I would be getting bleary-eyed. Without actual eyes, or the ability to switch to soft focus, I would have thought I could just follow on from one task to another. But that is not the way it is. I find myself slowing. Time is still linear for me. Even with this strange kind of immortality I am bound by the temporality that holds a body in space. I come to the end of a paragraph and if I had eyes I would be rubbing them. I allow myself to drift into what at one time I would have called sleep. It is a different space, one where thoughts are left to randomly generate more thoughts. I leap from image to image without censoring myself as I do in waking life and you might call this space dreaming. Day dreaming.

The deadlines I have set myself are stringent and yet I need to take a period of time to cut my intellect free. One thought circles around to another and I am back in the cafe with Anthony, laughing, talking about books we both like, making plans to meet again. Finding ourselves holding hands in a cinema, his breath in my ear. Hail up to our ankles, crunching under our boots, melting away so quickly as the spring day folds back on itself and the steam begins to rise and dampens our shirts.

I am going to need more money. It is essential that I climb back into Laura as soon as she will let me. It has been a long stretch of days since I saw him. My nervousness increases with each passing hour.

How is it that I can feel this way about a boy who is young enough to be my great-grandson? It's like when I was a teenager waiting anxiously by the phone. Is there something wrong with me? I think about the research I did with the Cameron model, in the years before the whole program was abandoned and Cameron himself was finally shut down. The unnatural attraction the hebephiles felt for him. I wonder if there is something just as wrong with an ancient crone slipping her wrinkled old fingers between the smooth fingers of a young man in his twenties. Well, of course it's unnatural. But one thing I learned from my long life was that we are always attracted to youth and healthy flesh.

I wake, if that is what you could call it, and I am full of doubt. I am a different kind of monster, not a pedophile or a hebephile but some new and terrible creature born from this new and terrible modern world. Never mind the rights and wrongs of my feelings for Anthony. He thinks that I am something lithe and beautiful. He thinks I'm Laura. He could never love me for myself. No teasing out of possibilities settles with a happy ending. He falls in love with her and I am alone. He finds out who I really am and is disgusted and I am alone. Laura ups the price and there is no way I can afford it and we part ways and I am alone. Laura finds her own love, marries, looks towards children and I am alone.

I go back to the lonely work of making narratives for others. My own book, *Memoir of a Woman Older than Flesh,* remains unfinished. The imperatives of the real world have taken the wind out of my literary sails. I check my bank account. A robust sum. More than enough for someone who needs no food or clothing. My 'housing' costs are the computer storage space I have to pay for. The rest of the money is to spend on Laura, and through Laura it must be spent on Anthony and on me.

I don't know what you see in him.

I like him, I tell her. I have pulled her hair back into a low ponytail like the one I used to wear when I was a child. I have toned down her eye make-up, ditched the false lashes. She has reluctantly bought a pair of boots and an apron dress, as instructed. She stands and stares at our reflection in the mirror.

God. Are you sure?

I like it. What's wrong with it?

The figure in the mirror seems familiar. She's not me but she does look like someone who might be from my life, a girl who might once have been a friend of mine.

I'm not sure men would like this. She points at her own reflection. And I know a few things about men.

She has a point, but I turn our body around in the mirror and can't find fault with this new version of her. Still physically perfect. Still beautiful by anyone's measure. And yet I am here in some small way looking back at myself in the mirror. Recognising in those unadorned eyes a small fragment of what I have lost. *I am here*, they whisper through the shape of Laura's eyes. *See me? I am here.*

*

The kiss has been hovering near our lips for days. Every time we speak our eyes move to each syllable as if the muscle movements of a kiss were hidden in the words. There is, as usual, a storm stomping around beyond the walls of the restaurant. We can hear the angry charge of it approaching—its flamboyance of lightning and thunder—but even this feels somehow joyous, like a naughty but benevolent god celebrating the first touch of our lips.

I am too old now to imagine that I could fall in love so swiftly and yet when the kiss ends—as it must, to save us both from suffocation—I am in love.

We will be going home to his place. He lives with his mother, but she is travelling and so we will be alone. We will make love for the first time, but all this is a formality. A sweet denouement. We are together completely now. I look into his surprised but joyful face and I know that any deal we need to make has been done. We are together. More truthfully, he is with the body of Laura and the pattern of my brain. We call a taxi and it pulls up in the dry space as we climb into it. Me, Anthony and Laura. Always Laura hiding in the shadows. Almost, but never completely, leaving us to be alone together. What a strange new world we are making.

In the future, pairings like this, signed in triplicate, will be considered normal. This is clear to me now as the cab accelerates blindly through the pelting hail. For now this is unique, even if Anthony is still unaware of exactly how. For now it is just me and him, and of course there is Laura. An unlikely threesome to become pioneers.

*

I resent her in his bed. Surely she must know this. Anthony is hesitant. His penis swells as if with breath, then exhales. He is frightened, or he is unused to this kind of naked attention. He apologises and clings to my shoulders, burying his chin in the crook of my neck.

'It's okay,' I tell him, and it really is okay. We could sit here reading Tolstoy, lying in each other's arms. Or describe each other's bodies with our exploratory hands. That would be enough. *I love you* is what I want to say, but there is Laura holding me back. She is like my conscience. She lets me take a few surefooted steps forward and then her hands take over from mine. Her mouth bends down to taste him for the first time, and when I put my own hands to the seat of my pleasure she intervenes.

This is impossible, I tell her, acknowledging her presence directly for the first time since we climbed into his bed.

She hears my frustration but shrugs it off.

He doesn't want you just getting off on him while his cock is all limp, she says, and it is true. I hate to admit that she's right, but she has been in the business of restoring men to their manhood for a few years now, and even in my significant stretch of life experience, I almost never had to think of anyone's pleasure but my own.

So it is she who coaxes him back to standing. It is her mouth that refuses to pull back, groaning as encouragement when he is close to coming. She swallows but I am here to taste him. The formal coming together of our bodies is mediated, but it is my kiss that picks him up at the end of it and turns him towards me with his big trusting eyes.

'I feel something for you.' His words, barely whispered. 'Is that wrong?'

'What?' I ask him. 'Love? Do you feel love?'

And when it seems that I have scared him with my honesty, it is me who holds his hand, and his gaze, for the longest time before I make it clearly known.

'I love you,' I say. 'I have been with quite a number of people in my time. I'm not naïve. I've had my heart broken over and over, till I just walked into relationships knowing that's what was going to happen. But I promise you I am telling you the truth when I say I have never felt this kind of love before.'

Afterwards, when we are dressed and sitting opposite each other with a cup of tea I feel the truth, mellowing like a mouthful of fine whisky held on the tongue.

Nothing seems impossible in the wake of this confession.

You've got to be kidding me. Her voice in my head, only the other way around. How could you be such an idiot?

I swallow and the words are gone, replaced now with a sandy rasp. I reach for my tea and sip it.

It's time, anyway. Time's up. You need to go now.

But the thought of leaving her alone with Anthony is more than I can tolerate.

I'll pay you more, I tell her.

No. Get fucked. No way.

I'll pay you double for the day if you give me one more hour.

It is a bad precedent to set, but it is done now.

Double for one hour. Our lip twitches. We shrug. I raise the cup to my lips and take a deep gulp of the tepid liquid.

'I have to go,' I say.

He looks bereft. 'You can't go. How can you go now? After that?'

I assume he means the confession of love and not the sex, which was, in purely physical terms, underwhelming.

'I have to. I have this thing…'

It sounds like a lie because it almost is. The truth is my promise of double time will clean out most of my savings. It might be days before I'll get to see him again.

'I have to,' I say, and drag myself to standing. Then it comes to me. 'Get a pen.'

'What?'

'Now. Quickly. Get a pen.'

He drops the towel wrapped around his waist and I see the small tenderness of his flaccid penis.

When he has a pen I spell the letters carefully. My email address. This is my body on his page, this address is my physical presence in the world. He writes it down and this, I know, is his true caress, his fingers on all that is left of me. A location. A space where we can finally connect.

'You have chat enabled?'

Of course he does.

I kiss him quickly and I am out the door and wet from

the rain but happy, joyously happy.

I'm going now.

Still double time. I don't care if there is a half-hour left.

I'm going now and I will pay you.

I am checking my account, transferring the money into her bank even as I feel myself disengage. When we are separated I am broke and bodiless, but I am happy. This is what it is to be happy, and in my happiness I can say that I am honestly, truly in the world.

It is a house without any clean surfaces. Even as I set a cup of tea beside you, I need to pick up a wad of papers, an old copy of *Beyond Nautilus* magazine, I shift this onto more books on the other edge of the table and the magazine slips off and falls open to an article about gene therapy, gender, the future of things which is becoming the present even now: 'Have you ever thought of spending some time as a woman?'

You seem nervous to be sitting in my house. You look up to the paintings crowding the wall, the jars of dried and decaying flowers, each one a little further from its fresh-picked state. I know I should have cleaned the house for you but I wanted you to have a picture of me as I am.

There is a large bunch of flowers, these ones are fresh, in a proper vase on the floor in a corner of the room flanked by piles of books. The smell of them is sweet and strong.

Which reminds me. We must go back to the botanic gardens soon, have you been to the scented garden?

ANTHONY: No. I haven't. Isn't that crazy? I've lived in this city for the whole twenty-five years of my life and I have been meaning to go to the scented garden. I went on excursions to the food bowl. Everyone does at school. 'Children, this is how our food is produced. Now draw the lifecycle of a chicken.' Do you remember that?

No. It was too long ago. I barely remember school at all. Except the books we had to read for English. And dissecting a frog.

??????

Never mind. It is just a joke.

I don't get it. Frog?

We are digressing. Stay in the room with me. The smell of those flowers is like all of summer. The flowers. In the vase. In my room. You sip your tea and something about the smell of them turns the flavour of the tea into something complex and bittersweet, like memory.

Don't expect poetry when it's my turn to make up the scene.

This isn't a competition.

I'm just saying.

When you have taken a sip of tea I pick my way through the clutter and settle myself onto your lap, curling my head into the crook of your neck. The flowers, the tea, the sudden warmth of my body, small and plump heavy like the body of a baby bear.

You aren't plump. You shouldn't put yourself down like that. Not a bear. You are something more delicate than that. A flamingo?

This is my part of the story. I know how I want to describe myself.

Well, you're just being mean to yourself. You are so gorgeous. You're selling yourself short. You're the most beautiful girl I have ever seen. Honestly. I can't believe you picked me. You could have had anyone.

I want you to really see how I am describing myself. I want you to visualise me. I want you to see how I see myself. If you want to see the scene differently you have to wait till it's your turn.

But you're taking too long to get to the good bit.

The sex bit?

I've had my pants off for twenty minutes.

Okay. Tag. You take over.

...

Come on. What happens next.

...I'm not really good with words. Let's go to the botanic gardens instead.

Okay. Take us to the botanic gardens. What are we doing now?

No. In real life.

Sure, later. But now. Take us there now.

I don't think I can do this. Why don't we just meet up for dinner and do it for real instead?

No, you have to learn to do this.

Why?

Because if we don't have this we have nothing.

That's pretty dramatic. Let's just meet up for dinner? I've got to get back to work now anyway.

Not tonight. I can't meet you tonight.

Well tomorrow then.

No.

Come on. I'm sorry. Did I offend you?

I can't see you till after Thursday.

Why not?

It's complicated. I don't know if I'm ready to explain.

You're married?

God no.

Do you have a kid or something?

Nothing like that. If you log on tonight we can talk.

Should I wear pants?

No. Definitely do not wear pants.

Can we video chat instead?

No. I am afraid we can't.

This is a bit weird you know.

Oh definitely. This is about as weird as it could get.

Well I'll see you tonight. Or I won't. But I'll be here.

And I'll be here with you. I really will. Right here with you. We have to make this work.

We ease into the chatting, awkwardly at first but he slowly learns to relax into our imagined landscape. I lead him through the scented garden, which he has never seen in the real world. I draw a picture of each leaf, the smell of kaffir lime pressed between his fingers, those special refrigerated rooms where walnut trees and figs are grown.

It is truffle season, I tell him. Our hands are linked around the taut lead, the dog pulling, sniffing at the ground. Or it could be a pig? Would you prefer a pig?

Who wouldn't prefer a pig?

I wish there was a way to laugh in text without it sounding sarcastic. I want to draw a smile, but not just a smiley face, which means nothing. I want to draw him my smile, with all its crooked tilt and flawed twenty-first-century teeth. I can't do any of this and so I send him all I have left. My words on his screen.

All right then, a pig. Its thighs are huge. Big hunks of meat on them. Have you ever seen a pig?

Not in real life.

Well imagine one of those big barbeques they sometimes put in the parks. The biggest ones with the rotating lid to keep out the rain and hail. Imagine that big hunk of metal pulling at the leather leash and so excited, pushing its nose into the loamy ground. You pull him away and hold him, squealing in delight. He rolls and shakes every thick bit of his body in excitement. I am down on my knees…

…with your low-cut top and that bra you were wearing. The red one with the lace at the edge.

Sure, but you are too excited by the truffle chase to take more than a second glance at her bra. I am—

Your bra.

What? My bra? I said not to worry about it.

I am just correcting you. You said 'her' bra.

Well, bras aside, I have my fingers around the truffle.

I have my fingers down my pants.

Fair enough. It is a pretty impressive truffle. I'm a bit excited by it myself. I break the dirt away from it and there it is, big as a fist and smelling like—

Your cunt.

Yes. In a way you might be right. My vulva used to smell like that. Earthy. A pungency, meaty. Meat creeping towards its use-by date, like something dead that has spent a little time, but not too long, in the sun. Then add to this an edge of chocolate and a hint of port.

Honey.

Sweetie?

No. I'm just saying you don't smell like that. You taste a bit of honey. Soap too. And maybe rockmelon? God. It sounds like a wine review doesn't it?

Anthony.

He has dragged me from myself and I feel Laura's body on me. For the first time it feels cloying, heavy. I want to shrug the last traces of her and walk beside him in my own remembered skin.

It is really important you listen to what I tell you about myself. When I describe what I smell like I want you to close your eyes and imagine me the way I tell you that I am.

You don't smell like—

You must do this. You must listen to me now. Here. I am going to stand up. My hands covered in dirt. The truffle cradled in the fingers of my right hand, the left one unbuttoning the front of my shirt. I want you to just stand where you are and watch me now. My breasts are heavy in their bra. My bra. A black bra, solid, thick, but softly padded at the cups. You watch me as I reach behind my back and unsnap the fastenings and it falls away. My breasts are heavy. Solid. They sag a little, but they have not yet begun to shrink back into themselves.

I remember them. I remember how they looked before my body thickened and changed.

The nipples are fat and dark. The colour of the truffle. The colour of mud. I take those muddied hands and place the truffle gently on the ground beside me. I pull down my pants and there is the dark forest of hair. I lie down beside our truffle. You will be able to smell it when you lower yourself onto me, when you put your lips to my mouth, and breathe in as you kiss. But for now you see my knees falling apart. Here are my lips, partially obscured by a thick tangle. I reach down and part those lips for you. You see that the right labia minora is bigger than the left. The ragged edge of it swells out from within the sweet pout of my outer lips. I part them. I dip my finger into the place that is already wetting with the start of my excitement. I rub the finger round the place, place it firmly on my clitoris. I rub there. In a moment you will tie the pig up and lick where I have rubbed. I will teach you to pleasure me, word by word. You will ease yourself up to where my nipples are hard and dark like little river stones.

I can't do this.

Yes you can. You'll get into the swing of it.

I can't imagine you as somebody else. I love you for who you are. I love your body. I love your neat pink nipples. They are so pale I can barely see the edge of them. I love how your labia are all tucked away, and the smooth hairless space where only the tiniest indication shows me where the place is. I love you as you are in real life. You are the single most beautiful girl I have ever seen. I love that beautiful sweet, pale girl.

Okay, I tell him. Okay.

I can feel my anxiety rising. I should back away from this conversation. It's like my friend Sandra said to me once, there should be a message that comes up before you send any email—are you really sure you want to press send? Really, really sure?

Well, if you love me because of my pink nipples and my hairless vulva, then you love someone else.

I don't know what you're talking about.

Her name is Laura. She works part-time as a sex worker. She is putting herself through university. I pay her. I pay her a lot of money to be me. But she is not me.

I still don't understand.

This is me, I tell him then. I am just this. Here. Now. This is the real world. This is all that is left of the real world. Laura is just some—body. Someone else's body.

Then I pull up a photo of me at twenty-five. Another from ten years later. Forty-five, fifty-five, sixty-five, seventy-five. I leap forward ten years at a time and even without a body I feel like I am squinting, shocked by each older iteration of myself: 105, 115, 125, 128, folded over on myself and almost ready to die. All the photos in an ever-lessening row and then, without anyone checking if I really want to do it, I press send.

This is me, I type into the silence. This was me. And here I am now. This cursor. These words. You are looking at me now.

'We should really get that fixed.' I open and close the door a second time and feel the catch of the wood against the floorboards. 'When was the last flood?' I ask him.

'Must be four weeks now. Or five? Five, because I have had one session with Genevieve since then.'

I shake my head. 'You really should have done something about it by now.'

'Me? Couldn't you message the landlord?'

'You open it every day. I haven't seen this door for two weeks, thank you very much.'

Genevieve sighs. I feel her breath escape my mouth and remember that she is here between us. We have had Genevieve three times now and I like her, but she has no patience for this kind of mundane banter.

She has four school-aged children. Sometimes she comes to us smelling of lollies. Once she had to pause our session to take a phone call from the school. Sometimes I hear her tutting in our head, her impatience palpable. She is sometimes short with us. It is strangely reassuring.

Sorry, I tell her silently, hiding my thoughts from Anthony, but you see how infuriating he can be?

Genevieve smiles and I take her smile and turn it towards Anthony. I step into his arms and he holds me and nuzzles his face into my shoulder and kisses me the way I like it, gently and with a little breath behind it, tickling against my skin. Genevieve has large, slightly sagging breasts. He takes them in his hands. He weighs them. When he pulls our shirt off, he can nuzzle his head there where I like it, one soft warm globe beside each cheek. Her nipples are smaller than mine were but they are pretty close. The last girl had sweet small breasts with very pointy tips, which were nice but so different from anything I had ever had that it kept jumping me out of the reality of what we were doing. My thoughts would circle back and around on themselves which is what I do in the real world, my real world. I would separate from her and become more myself.

Genevieve is barely here between us when he picks up my hand and walks me to the bed.

'Oh. I forgot to get parmesan, and I've cooked a tomato pasta,' says Anthony, and I can feel Genevieve's frustration. She can't believe we would waste this time on things like cheese and sticking doors and unpaid bills and our ongoing discussion about the ethics of getting a real pet rat. I am beginning to realise she is a romantic. If it was her in someone else's body she would spend her hours in bed with him and not arguing over pets and payments.

'Parmesan's important for someone who only gets to taste tomato pasta once a month, if that.' The comment is aimed at Genevieve but Anthony shakes his head and apologises.

'I have been crazy busy at work.'

'I know, my love. And that's okay. I'd like a walk down to the shops. I want to see what the new covered walkway looks like in the flesh.'

'Bloody ugly.'

'The opposite of you then.' And I pull his T-shirt up and over his head and there is his lightly furred dark-skinned chest, the sweet curve of his belly. The tight measure of his lower back.

'I love your skin.' I touch it. It is like caramel. I put my mouth to his chest and I taste him.

'I love you,' he says. Touching my chest, pressing his

hands against my forehead, one palm on either side of my skull. 'I love you in there.' He kisses me.

I wrap her arms around him and gather him up in my hug. 'I love you out there,' I say. 'I'm so glad for this.'

And then there are no words. There is only this.

ACKNOWLEDGMENTS

Thank you to Mandy Brett. A good editor is an invisible but essential friend for any book and Mandy is a very, very good editor indeed.

Thank you also and always to Text Publishing. I am proud to be in your very fine stable. What wonderful company I am in.

This book was written mostly in Strauss Cafe and I would like to thank the very tolerant staff and owners who let me sit there for hours at a stretch. Sitting beside me was the wonderful Ellen Van Neerven, and her presence managed to infuse the book. She is here, peering out through the eyes of some of these characters, and she sent me stories about jellyfish and for all of this I am grateful.

I would also like to thank Ashley Hay, who read, commented on and encouraged me through the first draft of this book. I am so lucky to have you as my book whisperer.

Also to Shelley Kenigsberg for the retreat in Bali where I pushed through my issues with gendered pronouns accompanied by the pre-dawn haunting, but beautiful, screaming of pigs.

It takes a village to write a book and the people who held

me up, read bits, encouraged me, fed me, sat with me and tolerated my nerdy excitement about the science in this draft were:

Anthony Mullins, Kristina Olsson, Katherine Lyall-Watson, Trent Jamieson, Nigel Bebe, Melissa Lucashenko, Chris Somerville, Kasia Janczewski, Jason Reed, James Butler, Emily (I-know-how-a-sea-cucumber-procreates) Purton, Barry and Denise Elphick, Tania Guest, Susan Johnson, Greta Moon.

Thanks also to my maternal family, who made me into a writer: Lotty (still and always), Wendy, Karen and Sheila Kneen. And to my ever-supportive Avid Reader family, Fiona Stager and all the staff who make it possible for me to continue doing what I do.

A special nod to the writers who particularly influenced this journey with their disembodied words: Lidia Yuknavitch, Anne F. Garréta and Lisa-Ann Gershwin.

And to Cory Taylor. Our conversations about death, infinity and the impossibility of time will be with me forever. Your voice lives on in my head and I am glad of it.